MORTAL GODS

Unseen Angels: The icons of selfless Giving

Exploring Living Gods and Extraordinary Figures

BEING A LIVING GOD

By

N.K.Sondhi

Editor Dr. Shruti Kohli

Rajmangal Prakashan

An Imprint of **Rajmangal Publishers**

ISBN : 978-9348578815

Published by :

Rajmangal Publishers

Rajmangal Prakashan Building,
1st Street, Ozone, Quarsi, Ramghat Road
Aligarh-202001, (UP) INDIA
Cont. No. +91- 7017993445
www.rajmangalpublishers.com
rajmangalpublishers@gmail.com
sampadak@rajmangalpublishers.in

प्रथम संस्करण : दिसम्बर 2024 – पेपरबैक

प्रकाशक : राजमंगल प्रकाशन

राजमंगल प्रकाशन बिल्डिंग, 1st स्ट्रीट,

ओजोन, क्वार्सी, रामघाट रोड,

अलीगढ़, उप्र. – 202001, भारत

फ़ोन : +91 - 7017993445

First Published : Dec. 2024 - Paperback
Printed by : Thomson Press India Ltd, Repro India Ltd & Manipal Tech Ltd.
eBook by : Rajmangal ePublishers (Digital Publishing Division)

INDEX

Disclaimer

This book presents factual information on individuals who are revered as god-like figures by ordinary people. While the material is based on extensive research and publicly available sources, the interpretations and descriptions are my own. I have endeavoured to represent these figures and their contributions accurately, but readers should note that this book reflects my understanding and analysis. The perspectives offered are not intended to serve as definitive assessments but rather as a homage to these revered personalities. Any errors in interpretation are unintentional and remain my responsibility.

1. INTRODUCTION

Throughout history, brilliant minds like philosophers, scientists, writers, and inventors have shaped the world we live in. They didn't just make discoveries or write books—they changed the way people think and live. Albert Einstein, for example, helped us understand the universe with his scientific theories, and Marie Curie's research in radioactivity saved lives. Philosophers like Socrates and Confucius gave us wisdom about living a good life, and writers like Shakespeare and Tolstoy captured human emotions and experiences in their works.

These great people are remembered not just for their big achievements but for their relentless efforts to make the world better. They remind us of the power of the human spirit to create, inspire, and bring positive change.

Small Acts Matter Most

Big accomplishments by famous people are inspiring, but small acts of kindness by ordinary people are just as important. A simple act like helping someone cross the road, comforting a friend, or sharing food with a hungry person can have a huge impact. These small gestures may seem ordinary, but they show the best side of humanity—kindness and selflessness.

When you lend a hand to someone in need, even if they're a stranger, you're showing compassion and empathy. It doesn't matter where you come from; helping others connects us all as humans. Think about how you feel when someone helps you—grateful and comforted. That's the power of small acts of goodness.

Why Do Some People Always Help Others?

Have you ever wondered why some people are so kind and always ready to help others? It's usually because of a combination of their personality, upbringing, and experiences. Some people have a deep sense of empathy and compassion, allowing them to understand what others are going through. When they see someone struggling, they feel the urge to help, as if they can step into the other person's shoes. Many of them grew up in families where kindness and generosity were valued and encouraged from a young age, making these traits a natural part of who they are. For others, helping others brings a sense of personal fulfillment. They don't do it for praise or recognition but simply because it feels good to make someone's life a little brighter.

Gratitude also plays a big role. These individuals often realize how fortunate they are—whether through education, opportunities, or support—and they feel a strong desire to share their blessings with those who are less fortunate. Some people are naturally altruistic, with a personality that enjoys spreading positivity without expecting anything in return. Lastly, the influence of their community or social circle is significant. Being surrounded by kind and generous people inspires them to act in the same way, creating a ripple effect of goodness. All these factors come together to drive their selfless desire to help others.

Every time someone helps, no matter how small the act, they make the world a better place. Whether it's comforting a friend, helping in a disaster, or simply being kind, these acts create ripples of goodness. You too can make a difference—one small act at a time.

2. BRINGING SMILES

Tales of Small Acts with Big Impact"

In the hustle and bustle of modern life, filled with noise and the rush of everyday obligations, there exists a breed of unsung heroes - the living gods among us. These individuals, devoid of grand titles or magnificent profiles, tread silently, yet steadfastly, through the world, representing compassion and courage in their every action. They are the ones who rush to aid distressed, desolate, and helpless souls, often at the risk of their own lives. Their stories, though untold in the grand halls of fame, resonate deeply, etching themselves into the fabric of humanity.
Let's look at their amazing actions, where ordinary people become extraordinary through their selfless acts. Here are a few examples of such simple yet inspiring individuals.

a) Poor by money rich by heart

Ravi, a destitute man, struggled to make ends meet. Balancing the care of his elderly parents and two children proved to be a daunting task. Despite his skill as a carpenter, he lacked a permanent workshop, he used to taking on odd jobs for those in need of his services, such as furniture repairs and door and bed fixes. Unfortunately, his clients were often slow to pay. Despite his declining health, Ravi had no choice but to work tirelessly every day due to financial constraints.

One fateful day, as Ravi sought refuge from the unpredictable weather beneath a tree in the village, heavy rains suddenly upset the area. With no proper drainage system in place, the village was quickly flooded, and its residents scrambled to protect their belongings and lives.

When heavy monsoon rains caused flooding in the village, leaving many families stranded and homes submerged in water. The entire community was in a state of panic, started rushing towards places where they could find higher ground to save them.

Amidst the chaos, Ravi emerged as a example of hope and strength. Despite the flooding threatening his own humble house, he immediately sprang into action, rallying his neighbours to assist those most in need.

Ravi grabbed a makeshift raft and began navigating through the flooded streets, rescuing elderly residents, children, and anyone else who was trapped by the rising waters. With remarkable courage and determination, he ventured into the most dangerous areas, risking his own safety to save others.

Throughout the day and into the night, Ravi tirelessly continued his rescue efforts, wading through waist-deep water, often in complete darkness, to reach those in distress. His selflessness knew no bounds as he comforted frightened children, reassured anxious parents, and offered a helping hand to anyone in need.

Even as tiredness set in and the enormity of the task weighed heavily on him, Ravi remained steadfast in his mission, driven by an unwavering commitment to serving his community. His acts of heroism inspired others to join in the rescue efforts, turning a potentially catastrophic situation into a display of unity and compassion.

By the time the floodwaters began to recede, Ravi had helped rescue dozens of villagers and provided much-needed support to countless others. His bravery and selflessness in the face of adversity left an indelible mark on the hearts of the villagers, who regarded him as a true hero and a shining example of the power of human kindness.

Long after the floodwaters had subsided, Ravi's extraordinary act of courage and compassion continued to be celebrated and remembered as a testament to the incredible impact that one individual can have when they choose to put the needs of others above their own.

b) Shadows of Compassion"

In the busy city, where tall buildings tower over crowded streets, one person quietly makes a difference in the little unnoticed corners. Raj, a man of humble means, earns his livelihood as a street vendor under the unforgiving sun, yet by night, he transforms into something more—a silent guardian angel to those who wander in the shadows of society.

One fateful night, as rain poured down in gushes, Raj's path intersected with fate beneath the cold embrace of a bridge. There, amidst the relentless downpour, he fell upon Meera, a fragile soul teetering on the edge of despair. Without hesitation, Raj extended his hand, offering not just shelter from the storm but a glimmer of hope in the darkness.

With an umbrella held high, Raj escorted Meera through the labyrinth of alleyways, navigating the treacherous terrain of the city's underbelly. Despite the dangers lurking in every shadow, his unwavering compassion served as a guiding light, leading them to the safety of a nearby shelter where warmth and solace awaited.

But this act of kindness was not an isolated incident. For years, Raj has woven a habit of compassion, crossing the forgotten corners of the metropolis, offering sustenance to those who hunger, comfort to those who weep, and a listening ear to those whose voices have been silenced by the cacophony of urban life.

His deeds may never be heralded in bold headlines or celebrated with grand gestures, but to those whose lives he has touched, Raj remains a silent guard—an example of hope in the darkest of nights, a testament to the power of compassion amidst the shadows of indifference.

c) Glimmers in the Night"

Story of Sarah

As the sun dipped below the horizon, casting long shadows across the city streets, Sarah set out on her nightly mission. With a sense of purpose appearing upon her face, she navigated the labyrinth of alleys and sidewalks, her eyes scanning every nook and cranny for signs of life.

In the dimming light, she spotted a figure huddled beneath a threadbare blanket, settled in the corner of a deserted building. With cautious steps, Sarah approached, her heart heavy with empathy. "Hello there," she called softly, her voice a gentle melody in the quiet of the evening.

The figures stirred, lifting their head to meet her gaze. In the dim glow of the streetlamp, Sarah saw the weariness fixed upon their face, the lines of hardship traced upon their brow. Yet, beneath the layers of dirt and despair, there flashed a spark of hope—a hope of humanity that refused to be extinguished.

With a warm smile, Sarah reached into her bag, took out a sandwich and a bottle of water. "I thought you might be hungry," she said, her voice laced with kindness. The person's eyes widened in surprise, gratitude washing over their features like a gentle tide.

As they shared the simple meal, Sarah listened intently to their story—their struggles, their triumphs, their dreams. In that fleeting moment of connection, they were no longer strangers bound by circumstance; they were kindred spirits walking the path of life together.

And so, Sarah continued her journey into the night, her footsteps echoing against the pavement, each one a testament to her unwavering commitment to those in need. For in the darkness of the city streets, she found not despair, but hope—an example guiding her towards a brighter tomorrow for all.

Every evening, Sarah embarked on her mission armed with a bag filled with sandwiches, water bottles, and warm blankets. She sought out those who called the streets their home, offering not just sustenance but solace. With a smile that lit up the darkest corners, she listened to their stories, shared laughter, and wiped away tears. In her presence, they felt safe and at peace, even if only for a short while, away from their tough lives.

Story of Emily

Emily, with her gentle touch and kind eyes, tended to the wounds of the forgotten souls. Armed with basic medical supplies and boundless sympathy, she offered comfort in the face of pain. With each bandage she applied and each soothing word she spoke, she stitched together fragments of dignity, reminding them that they were not alone in their suffering.

Emily's journey into providing medical aid to the homeless began with a simple act of compassion. It was a cold winter night when she stumbled upon an elderly man shivering beneath a torn blanket, his weak body barely visible in the darkness.

Moved by a sudden surge of empathy, Emily approached him, her heart heavy with concern. "Are you okay?" she asked softly, her voice a gentle sound in the chilly air.

The man looked up, his eyes filled with gratitude and weariness. "I'm fine, just a bit cold," he replied, his words appearing with exhaustion.

Unwilling to accept his tolerant response, Emily reached into her bag, pulling out a spare jacket and a thermos of hot tea. "Here," she said, offering to him with a warm smile. "These might help keep you warm."

As the man accepted her gifts, Emily noticed the raw, red skin on his hands, evidence of the harsh conditions he endured each day. Without a second thought, she reached for the first aid kit she always carried with her, gently tending to his wounds with practiced care.

In that moment, something shifted within Emily—a sense of purpose awakening deep within her soul. She realized that while she couldn't change the world, she could make a difference, one small act of kindness at a time.

From that day forward, Emily made it her mission to provide medical aid to the homeless. Armed with basic supplies and boundless compassion, she ventured out into the streets each evening, offering comfort and care to those in need.

With each bandage she applied and each soothing word she spoke, Emily stitched together fragments of dignity, reminding the homeless that they were not forgotten—that their lives mattered, even in the face of adversity.

And so, Emily's healing hands became a example of hope in the darkness, illuminating the path towards a brighter tomorrow for all who crossed her path. For in her touch, they found not just physical relief, but a glimmer of humanity—a reminder that even in the midst of hardship, compassion has the power to heal.

d) Beneath the Sign of Kindness"

Ramlal's grocery store is really popular with customers. Ramlal himself sets fair prices for everything in his store, and the stuff he sells is really good quality. Because his prices are fair and the goods are good, lots of people always come to his store. Ramlal is known for being honest and sticking to his prices without haggling. He's so busy that he can't negotiate prices with customers, so he put up a sign saying he doesn't give discounts.

Near Ramlal's store, there's a man named Jai Singh who's really poor. He works as a daily labour in construction, but because the city banned construction due to pollution, he couldn't find work for a long time. He used up all his savings, and one day, he didn't have any money left to buy food for his family. Jai Singh remembered he had a golden ring his father-in-law gave him when he got married, so he decided to sell it for money. Unfortunately, he got cheated and only got half of what the ring was worth.

With the money he got, Jai Singh went to Ramlal's store to buy food, but he was short by ten rupees. He asked Ramlal for a discount because he couldn't afford the full amount, and he explained his situation, saying he hadn't eaten in two days. Ramlal, even though he usually doesn't give discounts, thought for a moment and then sent someone to bring food for Jai Singh and his family. Not only did Ramlal give him food to eat right away, but he also arranged enough food for a whole week for Jai Singh's family. Ramlal said he wouldn't compromise his business principles, but he believed in helping others in need.

e) Mountain Task – Carving a hope for others

Dashrath Manjhi, also known as the "Mountain Man," was a remarkable individual from India who single-handedly carved a path through a mountain using only a hammer and chisel. His story is one of extraordinary perseverance and determination.

Manjhi was born into a poor family in the Gehlaur village of Bihar, India, in 1934. His village was situated at the base of a massive rocky hill, and the nearest town and resources were located on the other side. The villagers had to travel around the mountain, which was a journey that took hours, to access medical facilities, schools, and other essential services. This geographical barrier had a significant impact on their lives.

In 1959, tragedy struck when Manjhi's wife, Falguni Devi, fell ill. Due to the lack of prompt medical attention caused by the mountain's obstruction, she passed away. This event deeply affected Manjhi, and he vowed to break through the mountain to prevent others from suffering the same fate as his wife.

Despite being mocked and ridiculed by fellow villagers for his seemingly impossible ambition, Manjhi was undeterred. Armed with only a hammer, chisel, and his unwavering determination, he began his monumental task. Day after day, for over two decades, Manjhi tirelessly chipped away at the rocky terrain, gradually carving out a narrow passage through the mountain.

Manjhi's efforts were nothing short of miraculous. He worked tirelessly, often enduring harsh weather conditions and physical exhaustion. His determination captured the attention of the media and eventually the government, which provided him with assistance and recognition.

Finally, in 1982, after 22 years of relentless labour, Dashrath Manjhi succeeded in his mission. He had carved a road 360 feet long, 30 feet wide, and 25 feet high, reducing the travel distance between his village and the nearest town from 55 kilometers to just 15 kilometers.

Manjhi's incredible feat not only transformed the lives of the people in his village but also inspired countless others around the world. He became a symbol of resilience, showing that with unwavering determination and hard work, seemingly insurmountable obstacles can be overcome.

Dashrath Manjhi's legacy lives on as a testament to the power of human perseverance and the ability to make a difference, even in the face of seemingly impossible odds. He passed away in 2007, but his extraordinary story continues to inspire generations to come.

f) The Unity of Shoeshine

Once, at a railway station, a few gentlemen were waiting for their train when a shoe shiner approached one of them and asked, "Sir, shall I polish your shoes?"

Seeing his pitiable condition, he extended his shoes and replied, "Sure, but do it properly."

The boy began his work, but unlike other shoe shiners, he lacked enthusiasm. The passenger exclaimed, "Why are you working so sluggishly? Hurry up!"

The boy remained silent.

In the midst of this, another boy arrived. He immediately separated the first boy and got to work promptly. The first boy stood aside silently while the second boy shined the shoes.

"Who should I pay?" he wondered, reaching for his pockets. He thought, "There might be an argument or fight between these two for the payment." So, he decided, "The one who did the job deserves the payment." Consequently, he gave the money to the second boy.

He accepted the money but placed it in the first boy's palm. With affection, he patted his back and left.

The man watched in astonishment. He promptly called the second boy back and asked, "What's going on?"

The boy explained, "Sir, three months ago, he fell off a moving train. He was severely injured in his hands and legs. Fortunately, he survived, but what about his elderly mother and sisters? He's too proud to beg."

Then, pausing, he continued, "Sir, the shoe shiners here form our own group, and among us, there's a beloved elder whom we affectionately call 'Uncle.' He goes to spiritual gatherings and shares those teachings with us. It was he who suggested, 'Friends, if we can't work with enthusiasm like before, then what? God has given us an opportunity to demonstrate active goodwill, sacrifice, love, compassion, and unity towards our fellow beings, just as the different parts of the body, like the back, stomach, face, hands, and feet, though appearing different, are part of the same body. Similarly, though we may appear different, we are one soul. We are all one.'

We, the residents of this station, decided together that we will contribute our earnings from polishing one pair of shoes daily and assist each other when needed."

Witnessing such heights of mutual love, cooperation, unity, and humanity among the shoe shiners, the gentleman was amazed and felt joyous. He patted his back in return and began to ponder, perhaps humanity is still alive...!

g) The Cart of Compassion

In an Indian village settled within fields of green, a humble handcart labourer was going along the dusty road, his cart laden with goods for market. As the sun beat down mercilessly, he wiped sweat from his brow, and hoped to reach his destination shortly.

Amidst the ordinary style of his day, fate intervened in the form of an unconscious person lying by the roadside. Though many passers-by glanced at the fallen individual, none extended a helping hand. But this labourer, with compassion in his heart, halted his cart and approached the stricken person.

Upon examination, he found faint signs of life—breath but no words. Without hesitation, he decided to help the stranger. Attempts to flag down passing vehicles proved futile. So, with determination, he lifted the unconscious soul onto his cart, intent on seeking medical assistance. Yet, in this rural expanse, the nearest doctor or clinic lay distant and inaccessible.

Undeterred by the challenges, he made a daring choice—to bring the stranger home. Through winding paths and rough land, he navigated his cart, each bump and jolt was a proof to his firm decion.

For days, the labourer set aside his livelihood, devoting himself to the care of his unexpected guest. He tended to his needs tirelessly—feeding, cleansing, and soothing his pains. Through his selfless dedication, the stranger gradually regained strength, returning from the brink of oblivion.

In the absence of the labourer's intervention, the stranger might have succumbed to the cruel indifference of fate. But through his actions, this ordinary man surpassed his position, exemplifying the spirit of divinity—a living god among mortals.

h) Shadows in the Night

One chilly winter's night, as the city lay shrouded in darkness, a young woman named Maya found herself alone and afraid in a desolate lane. She had lost her way while walking home from work and had stumbled into a dangerous part of town, where the shadows seemed to loom menacingly and danger lurked around every corner.

Just as Maya's fear threatened to overwhelm her, a soft voice broke through the silence, offering words of reassurance and guidance. Startled, Maya looked up to see a figure covered in darkness standing before her, her presence radiating a sense of calm and protection.

"Are you lost, miss?" the stranger asked, her voice gentle yet commanding.

Trembling, Maya nodded, her eyes wide with fear. She had heard tales of danger loitering in the streets at night, and now she found herself living one.

Without hesitation, the stranger extended a hand to Maya, offering to escort her safely home. Maya was thankful for the help and felt relieved as she followed the stranger through the confusing streets of the city.

As they walked, the stranger shared stories of her experiences, recounting tales of bravery and compassion that had earned reputation as a helpful neighbour. Maya listened in awe, feeling inspired by the stranger's selflessness and determination to make a difference in the lives of others.

But amidst their conversation, Maya noticed something peculiar—a warmth emanating from the stranger's presence, as if her kindness had lit a fire in the darkness of the night. She couldn't help but feel a sense of comfort and safety in her company.

Finally, they reached Maya's doorstep, and she turned to thank the stranger for her kindness and guidance. But before she could speak, the mysterious figure had vanished into the night, leaving Maya with a sense of wonder and gratitude that would stay with her forever.

In the days that followed, Maya couldn't shake the memory of her encounter with the stranger. She found herself drawn to the lanes and streets where they had walked together, searching for traces of her presence. But the stranger remained elusive, a silent guardian watching over the city from the shadows.

Yet, Maya felt a newfound sense of courage and determination stirring within her. Inspired by the stranger's example, she dedicated herself to helping those in need, whether it be offering food to the homeless or lending a listening ear to those who were hurting.

And as she walked the streets of the city, Maya couldn't help but feel the warmth of the stranger's presence, guiding her every step of the way. For in the darkness of the night, their light shone brightest, an example of hope and compassion for all who were lost and afraid.

i) Threads of Compassion

In the dark of night, tragedy struck a small child, leaving him orphaned by the cruel hands of fate. His parents, the pillars of his world, were snatched away in a heart-wrenching road accident, leaving him utterly alone, except for a distant relative. But what should have been a helping hand in his despair soon turned into a nightmare of exploitation.

Under the guise of familial obligation, the relative took the child into his home, promising to nurture him as his own. Yet, as time passed on, the child began to feel his existence as nothing more than an unpaid servant. Every boring task, from scrubbing clothes to scrubbing floors, fell upon his small shoulders. And for every mistake, not only was he met with harsh punishment, but he was also deprived of the basic sustenance of food.

The burden became unbearable, suffocating him with each passing day. The weight on him became too much to handle, making it harder for him every day. Then one night, in the quiet of the house, the child bravely ran away into the unknown. Alone and vulnerable, he sought refuge on the unforgiving streets, where survival became his sole purpose. Amid the busy and terrible traffic on the road, he came across a traveller whose car had crashed into a tree near a small roadside food stall. The driver was badly injured, lying in the wreckage, bleeding and crying for help, but his cries were filled with hopelessness. Not knowing what to do he, with trembling hands, he offered a simple glass of water. Thereafter he started crying loudly in the silence of the night for seeking help from other people. His desperate cries for help in the silence of the night brought good results. With the result many kind hearted people came to help the injured driver.

As the injured man was taken to safety, the child noticed a bag lying in the wreckage. Without thinking much, he took it, not knowing how valuable its contents were. Inside the bag were not just belongings but also items crucial to the car owner's life.

The next morning, when the owner came back looking for the bag, he found the child waiting with it. The child handed it over, untouched and exactly as it was. The owner's heart was filled with gratitude and admiration for the child's honesty and integrity.

Learning of the child's tragic past and the injustices he had endured, the owner was overcome with a profound sense of responsibility. Promises were made, not just of material comfort, but of a future filled with dignity and opportunity. And in that fleeting moment of connection, two souls found solace in each other's embrace, bound together by the threads of compassion and understanding. The child and the car owner both were like living gods for each other.

As days turned into weeks and weeks into months, the child found himself welcomed into the owner's home, not as a servant but as a cherished member of the family. He was given the opportunity to learn and grow, to pursue his dreams without fear or restraint.

And as he looked back on the darkest chapter of his life, the child realized that it was the kindness of a stranger that had saved him from despair. For in the midst of tragedy, he had found not only a guardian angel but a friend—a guiding light to lead him out of the shadows and into the warmth of a brighter tomorrow.

3.MORTAL GODS

In our society, some people stand out so much that they are admired and respected like gods. These extraordinary individuals, though human, have qualities or achievements that make them seem larger than life. This book explores why and how some people are treated like gods in their fields.

From great historical figures to modern icons, whether in science, entertainment, or other areas, we'll look at people whose names are spoken with admiration and whose work has left a lasting impact. Their talent, vision, and contributions make them special and unforgettable, filling us with wonder and respect.

But what is it that sets these individuals apart? What alchemy of talent, circumstance, and destiny propels them to such lofty heights? Are they mere mortals blessed with extraordinary gifts, or do they embody something superior, something divine?

In this exploration, we explore into the lives and legacies of doctors, scientists, artists, entrepreneurs, and leaders who have captured the collective imagination and earned the adoration of their peers and followers. We examine the qualities that distinguish them, the impact of their work on society, and the complex interplay of factors that contribute to their godlike status.

As we explore these stories of greatness, we also see the other side of idolizing people—the problems with blindly worshipping heroes, the risks of giving too much power to one person, and the fragile nature of human dreams. Even the greatest among us have flaws because they are still human.

4. DOCTORS

The Healing Touch
A Rural Tale of Compassion and Hope"

In the heart of a rural village in India, where the dusty roads wind between fields of golden wheat and lush greenery, there stood a modest clinic. Its walls, weathered by time and neglect, bore the scars of countless monsoons, its roof patched together with scraps of tin and tarpaulin. Here, amidst the simple surroundings, Dr. Arjun held sway, not just as a healer, but as a beacon of hope and compassion in the eyes of the villagers.

Life in this rural area was a daily struggle against the elements, against poverty, and against the relentless march of disease. For the needy people, access to healthcare was a distant dream, a luxury reserved for those with the means to afford it. Government hospitals were few and far between, their resources stretched thin by the overwhelming demand from neighbouring towns and cities. And so, the villagers were left to protect for themselves, relying on home remedies and folk medicine to treat their ailments.

One hot summer day, Rahul's parents were filled with worry and fear. Their only child, Rahul, was very sick. He had a high fever and was weak, and they couldn't help him get better at home. The village they lived in had no government hospitals or clinics. Because they were poor, they felt helpless as they watched their son's health get worse.

With fear and worry, they went to Dr. Arjun, whose reputation as a miracle worker had spread far and wide. As they crossed the threshold of his clinic, their hearts heavy with fear and uncertainty, they were met not by the cold indifference that often accompanies poverty, but by the warm embrace of compassion shining from Dr. Arjun's presence.

Inside the clinic, the scene was one of chaos and despair. The waiting room was filled to bursting with villagers, their faces filled with worry as they awaited their turn to seek solace from the good doctor. Some carried infants wracked with fever, while others supported elderly relatives crippled by age and infirmity. Each bore the scars of a life lived on the margins of society, their bodies worn down by years of toil and hardship.

With a gentle touch and a reassuring smile, Dr. Arjun took Rahul onto the examination table, his experienced hands probing for the source of the boy's suffering. Despite the severity of Rahul's condition, Dr. Arjun remained steadfast, his unwavering dedication to his patient a testament to his calling as a healer.

Days turned into weeks as Dr. Arjun tirelessly tended to Rahul's needs, his every action guided by a profound sense of empathy and understanding. The villagers watched in wonder as the once-ailing boy began to regain his strength, his fever breaking under the watchful care of the good doctor.

To Rahul and his family, Dr. Arjun was more than just a physician; he was a lifeline, a ideal of hope in their darkest hour. They spoke of him in respectful tones, likening him to a deity who walked among mortals, his healing touch a divine intervention that had saved their beloved son from the clutches of death.

Years passed, and Rahul grew into a robust young man, his once a weak body now a testament to the healing power of Dr. Arjun's compassion. Though the good doctor had long since departed from this world, his legacy endured, a reminder to all who knew him that greatness lies not in wealth or status, but in the simple acts of kindness and selflessness that define the human spirit.

In many societies, doctors are revered for their healing abilities and wisdom, often seen as "mortal gods" due to their profound impact on patients' lives. Their medical expertise allows them to cure diseases and restore health, earning them awe and gratitude. Beyond their skills, doctors' compassion provides comfort in times of fear and vulnerability, enhancing their godlike image. The life-or-death decisions they make and their dedication to patients' well-being reinforce this view. Doctors also serve as trusted advisors and community leaders, working to improve public health and earning respect akin to divine helpers.

In many communities, doctors are more than just medical professionals. They are trusted advisors, community leaders, and advocates for public health. They work on projects that improve the well-being of the entire community, earning admiration and respect akin to that given to divine helpers.

Sometimes, doctors achieve amazing results that seem like miracles. When patients recover from serious illnesses or injuries against all odds, it adds to the belief that doctors have special powers.

In summary, people see doctors as having godlike qualities because of their ability to heal, their knowledge, compassion, responsibility, and sacrifices. While they don't have supernatural powers, their role in easing suffering, restoring health, and guiding people through tough times earns them a place of respect and awe.

5. A TRIUMPH OF HUMANITY

The Story of Polio Medicine: A Triumph for Humanity

The Scourge of Polio

In the early 20th century, polio was one of the most feared diseases in the world. It struck suddenly, often affecting children, leading to paralysis, disability, and sometimes death. Communities lived in fear as epidemics would sweep through, leaving devastation in their wake. Hospitals were filled with iron lungs, large machines that helped polio victims breathe when their muscles failed them. It was a time when there was no effective medicine for Polio. When the polio wide spread with no medicine for treatment, it was a great Doctor Jonas Salk who ventured to find a vaccine for polio treatment.

A Visionary Scientist: Jonas Salk

The story of the polio vaccine begins with Jonas Salk, a young medical researcher with a keen mind and an unyielding determination. Born in 1914 in New York City, Salk was the son of Russian-Jewish immigrants. His early fascination with science and medicine led him to New York University, where he earned his medical degree.

During World War II, Salk worked on developing a vaccine for influenza, which laid the foundation for his future work. In 1947, he joined the University of Pittsburgh, where he began his ground-breaking research on polio. In the 1940s and 1950s, polio was a widespread and feared disease, especially affecting children. Salk and his team at the University of Pittsburgh developed the inactivated polio vaccine (IPV), which was introduced in 1955. Unlike earlier experimental approaches, Salk's vaccine used killed virus particles, making it both safe and effective.

The Quest for a Vaccine

Polio was caused by a virus, and scientists had different ideas about how to make a vaccine. Some thought a live virus should be used, while Jonas Salk believed using a killed virus would be safer and still work well. Salk's method involved growing the virus in a lab and then killing it with a chemical called formaldehyde. This made the vaccine safe because it helped the body fight the virus without causing the disease.

Salk and his team of hardworking researchers and technicians put in long hours, often staying late at night. They faced many difficulties, like making sure the virus was completely killed and figuring out how to produce the vaccine on a large scale. Despite these challenges, Salk stayed focused and determined to succeed.

By 1952, Salk had developed a promising vaccine. However, proving its effectiveness required large-scale testing. In 1954, the largest medical experiment in history was launched. Over 1.8 million children, dubbed "Polio Pioneers," participated in the double-blind, placebo-controlled field trials. The entire nation held its breath, waiting for the results.

On April 12, 1955, the results were announced: Salk's vaccine was safe and effective. The news was met with jubilation. Church bells rang, and people celebrated in the streets. The vaccine was hailed as a miracle, and Jonas Salk became a national hero.

The Impact on Humanity

The introduction of the polio vaccine had a profound impact on humanity. Polio cases dropped dramatically. Parents could finally breathe a sigh of relief, knowing their children were protected from the dreaded disease. The success of the vaccine also encouraged further advancements in medical research and vaccine development.

Salk chose not to patent the vaccine, ensuring it could be widely distributed and affordable. When asked who owned the patent, he famously replied, "There is no patent. Could you patent the sun?" This selfless act highlighted his commitment to public health over personal gain.

People think of Jonas Salk as a hero who changed the world with his work on the polio vaccine. In the 1950s, polio was a terrifying disease, especially for children. It paralyzed and even killed many people. When Salk and his team developed the first safe and effective vaccine, it brought hope and relief to millions.

What made Salk stand out wasn't just his science but also his kindness. He refused to patent the vaccine, even though it could have made him very rich. When asked why, he famously said, *"Could you patent the sun?"* This showed that he cared more about helping people than making money.

Salk's work made him a symbol of hope. Many admire him not only for saving lives but also for being selfless and putting humanity first. Even after the vaccine, he continued to work for the betterment of society, founding the Salk Institute to support scientific research.

Though some people later argued that other scientists, like Albert Sabin, also played a big role in fighting polio with their own vaccines, it doesn't take away from Salk's incredible contribution. Most people remember him as a humble, compassionate man who used science to make the world a better place.

A Legacy of Hope

The success of the polio vaccine opened the door for global efforts to wipe out the disease. Later, Albert Sabin developed an oral polio vaccine, which became widely used because it was easy to give, especially during mass vaccination drives. Together, these vaccines have nearly eliminated polio worldwide.

Today, polio exists in only a few countries, thanks to the hard work of global health organizations and volunteers. The story of the polio vaccine shows what we can achieve through science, teamwork, and determination. Jonas Salk's legacy lives on in the millions of lives saved and in the spirit of compassion and curiosity that continues to inspire medical research and public health efforts. His work reminds us that, with vision and perseverance, we can overcome even the toughest challenges and build a healthier future.

Doctors are often seen as heroes for their extraordinary contributions to medicine. For example, Alexander Fleming's discovery of antibiotics revolutionized how we treat bacterial infections, saving countless lives. Christiaan Barnard, who performed the first successful heart transplant in 1967, showed the incredible possibilities of surgery.

Through hard work, doctors have made breakthroughs that changed lives. Frederick Banting and Charles Best discovered insulin, giving hope to people with diabetes. John Snow's research during a cholera outbreak in 1854 helped create modern public health practices, saving lives by tracing the disease to contaminated water.

Emergency doctors like Peter Safar, who developed CPR, have equipped everyday people to save lives during heart emergencies. Psychiatrists like Sigmund Freud explored the human mind, helping people cope with mental illness.

Globally, doctors like Paul Farmer have worked tirelessly to provide healthcare in poor countries, showing the true meaning of humanitarian medicine. Leaders like William Osler, often called the "Father of Modern Medicine," shaped medical education, teaching the value of compassion and lifelong learning.

In all these ways, doctors have shown remarkable skill, dedication, and kindness, earning the respect and admiration of people everywhere. Their efforts to save and improve lives remind us of their vital role in societ

6. INNOVATIVE THINKERS AND INVENTORS

Mortal gods" are individuals who, through their extraordinary talents, achievements, or contributions, have garnered widespread admiration, respect, and sometimes even reverence from society. They transcend the ordinary and become symbols of greatness, often leaving an indelible mark on history or culture. In this chapter let's look at some examples:

Marie Curie

A pioneering physicist and chemist, Marie Curie was the first woman to win a Nobel Prize and the only person to win Nobel Prizes in two different scientific fields (Physics and Chemistry). Her ground-breaking research on radioactivity paved the way for advancements in medical treatment and nuclear physics, demonstrating the power of scientific inquiry to improve lives.

Born Maria Sokolowski on November 7, 1867, in Warsaw, Poland, she was raised in a family that prioritized education and intellectual pursuits despite facing adversity under Russian occupation. Marie's thirst for knowledge led her to pursue higher education, but being a woman in late 19th-century Poland presented significant challenges. Undeterred, she moved to Paris in 1891 to study at the Sorbonne, where she faced financial struggles but excelled academically. In 1895, she met Pierre Curie, a fellow physicist, and they soon married, forming a partnership that would change the course of scientific history. Together with Pierre, Marie embarked on research into the newly discovered phenomenon of radioactivity. In 1898, they isolated two new elements: polonium, named after Marie's native Poland, and radium. Their ground-breaking work earned them international acclaim and laid the foundation for modern nuclear physics.

In 1903, Marie Curie became the first woman to receive a Nobel Prize, sharing the honour with Pierre and physicist Henri Becquerel for their pioneering research on radioactivity. Tragically, Pierre died in a traffic accident in 1906, leaving Marie to continue their work alone. Despite facing discrimination as a female scientist, Marie Curie persevered, becoming the first woman to be appointed as a professor at the Sorbonne. In 1911, she received her second Nobel Prize, this time in Chemistry, for her discovery and characterization of radium and polonium.

Marie Curie's legacy extends far beyond her scientific achievements. She shattered gender barriers in academia and paved the way for future generations of women in science. Her work laid the groundwork for advancements in oncology, radiology, and nuclear medicine, saving countless lives through the diagnosis and treatment of cancer.

Marie's tireless dedication to science came at a personal cost. Her prolonged exposure to radioactive materials took a toll on her health, leading to chronic illness and ultimately contributing to her premature death. Yet, even in the face of adversity, she remained committed to her research and advocacy for the peaceful use of radiation in medicine.

Marie Curie's contributions to science and her enduring legacy as a trailblazing woman in STEM continue to inspire generations of scientists and scholars worldwide. She remains a symbol of perseverance, curiosity, and the transformative power of scientific inquiry.

Nelson Mandela

An iconic anti-apartheid revolutionary and politician, Nelson Mandela dedicated his life to fighting against racial injustice and promoting reconciliation and equality in South Africa. Despite enduring 27 years of imprisonment, Mandela emerged as a global symbol of resilience, forgiveness, and peace, leading his country through a peaceful transition to democracy and inspiring countless individuals around the world.

Nelson Mandela, born on July 18, 1918, in Mvezo, South Africa, faced apartheid's injustices(keeping people of different races separate) from an early age. Despite discrimination, he studied law at the University of Fort Hare and the University of Witwatersrand. In the 1940s, Mandela joined the African National Congress (ANC) and fought against racial segregation and oppression, providing legal counsel to those affected by apartheid laws.

The peaceful resistance led by Mandela faced violent repression from the South African government. The 1960 Sharpeville Massacre, where police killed 69 peaceful protesters, led Mandela to adopt more militant tactics. In 1962, he was arrested and sentenced to life imprisonment for advocating armed resistance. During his 27 years in prison, mostly on Robben Island, Mandela endured harsh conditions but remained a symbol of hope and resilience, inspiring the fight for freedom and equality within South Africa and globally.

Throughout his imprisonment, Mandela became a symbol for the anti-apartheid movement, gaining global support. His release in 1990 marked the end of apartheid and the start of a new era for South Africa. Following his release, Mandela played a crucial role in South Africa's transition to democracy. He led negotiations with the apartheid government and promoted reconciliation. In 1994, he was elected as South Africa's first black president in the first fully democratic elections, symbolizing the triumph of democracy.

As president, Mandela worked to dismantle apartheid's legacy by promoting national reconciliation, human rights, and economic development. He became a global icon of peace and earned the Nobel Peace Prize in 1993 for his efforts. Even after stepping down in 1999, Mandela continued to advocate for justice and equality until his passing on December 5, 2013. His legacy of freedom and social justice inspires many, highlighting the power of perseverance, forgiveness, and reconciliation.

There is an interesting story about Nelson Mandela's commitment to forgiveness and reconciliation. After becoming President of South Africa in 1994, Mandela embarked on a journey of healing and unity for a nation scarred by decades of apartheid. One notable incident occurred when Mandela visited a restaurant in Johannesburg. While dining, he noticed a white man, a former member of the apartheid-era security forces, sitting at a nearby table. This man had been a prison guard at Robben Island, where Mandela had spent much of his 27-year imprisonment. Instead of harbouring resentment or seeking revenge, Mandela approached the man with grace and compassion. He engaged him in conversation, and as they spoke, it became clear that the man recognized Mandela. Despite the man's past role in perpetuating the oppressive system of apartheid, Mandela chose to extend a hand of reconciliation rather than condemnation.

Mandela's ability to forgive his captors and oppressors exemplified his belief in the power of forgiveness and reconciliation to heal the wounds of the past and build a more inclusive and harmonious future for South Africa. This story has become emblematic of Mandela's legacy as a champion of forgiveness, reconciliation, and social justice, inspiring people around the world to strive for peace and understanding even in the face of adversity and injustice.

Mother Teresa

Mother Teresa, known as the "Saint of the Gutters," dedicated her life to serving the poorest of the poor in the slums of Kolkata, India, and around the world. Born Agnes Gonxha Bojaxhiu on August 26, 1910, in Skopje (now in North Macedonia), she felt a calling to become a nun from a young age. At the age of 18, she joined the Sisters of Loreto and travelled to India to begin her missionary work.

In Kolkata, Mother Teresa witnessed extreme poverty, suffering, and disease among the city's most vulnerable inhabitants. Motivated by her faith and a deep sense of compassion, she made it her life's mission to provide comfort and care to those in need, especially the sick, the homeless, and the dying.

In 1950, Mother Teresa founded the Missionaries of Charity, a religious group dedicated to serving "the poorest of the poor." The Missionaries of Charity soon grew into a global network of volunteers and charitable organizations, providing food, shelter, medical care, and love to millions of people in need.

Mother Teresa's work was characterized by humility, simplicity, and selflessness. She lived among the people she served, often attending to those who were rejected or forgotten by society. Her compassion knew no bounds, and she treated each person she encountered with dignity and respect, regardless of their circumstances.

Renowned for her selfless devotion to serving the poorest of the poor, Mother Teresa founded the Missionaries of Charity, a Roman Catholic religious flock that operates hospitals and homes for people with HIV/AIDS, leprosy, and tuberculosis, as well as orphanages and schools. Mother Teresa's extraordinary devotion to serving the side-lined earned her international recognition and numerous awards, including the Nobel Peace Prize in 1979. However, she remained humble and focused on her mission, directing attention away from herself and toward the plight of the poor and suffering.

Throughout her life, Mother Teresa remained committed to her vow of poverty, living simply and devoting herself entirely to the service of others. She once said, "It is not how much we do, but how much love we put in the doing.

It is not how much we give, but how much love we put in the giving."

Mother Teresa passed away on September 5, 1997, but her legacy of love, compassion, and service lives on through the Missionaries of Charity and the countless lives she touched. She is remembered as a beacon of hope and a symbol of selfless love, inspiring people of all faiths and backgrounds to dedicate themselves to helping those in need.

Albert Einstein

Albert Einstein is often respected as a scientific genius whose contributions to our understanding of the universe were monumental. While labelling him as a "mortal god on earth" might be inflated, it speaks to the profound impact he had on both science and society.

Einstein was born in Ulm, in the Kingdom of Württemberg in the German Empire, on March 14, 1879. His early life was marked by academic excellence, although he struggled in a traditional school environment. He later enrolled at the Polytechnic Institute in Zurich, where he studied physics and mathematics, eventually obtaining Swiss citizenship and his doctorate.

Einstein's breakthrough came in 1905, a year often referred to as his "miracle year," during which he published four ground-breaking papers in the field of theoretical physics. Among these was his theory of special relativity, which introduced the famous equation E=mc2E=mc^2E=mc2, demonstrating the equivalence of mass and energy. This theory revolutionized our understanding of space, time, and the relationship between matter and energy.

His subsequent work, including his theory of general relativity published in 1915, further reshaped modern physics. General relativity proposed a new understanding of gravity as the curvature of spacetime caused by mass and energy, offering predictions that were later confirmed through observations of gravitational lensing and the precession of Mercury's orbit.

In 1903, Einstein married Mileva Marić, a fellow physicist whom he met while studying at the Polytechnic Institute in Zurich. They had two sons together, Hans Albert and Eduard. However, their marriage faced significant challenges, and they eventually divorced in 1919.After his divorce, Einstein married his cousin Elsa Löwenthal in 1919. Elsa was supportive of Einstein's work and played a significant role in managing his affairs and correspondence. They remained married until her death in 1936.

Einstein's contributions extended beyond theoretical physics. He played a significant role in the development of quantum theory, although he famously clashed with some aspects of it, famously saying, "God does not play dice with the universe." He also made important contributions to the understanding of Brownian motion and the photoelectric effect, the latter of which earned him the Nobel Prize in Physics in 1921.

Despite his professional success, Einstein faced numerous personal struggles throughout his life. His first son, Hans Albert, experienced difficulties in school and in his relationship with his father. Eduard, Einstein's second son, struggled with mental health issues and spent much of his life in psychiatric institutions.

Einstein was known for his eccentricities and nonconformist lifestyle. He had a playful sense of humour and enjoyed playing the violin and sailing. He was also deeply passionate about social and political issues, advocating for pacifism, civil rights, and international cooperation.

In 1933, Einstein emigrated to the United States to escape the rise of Nazism in Germany. He settled in Princeton, New Jersey, where he accepted a position at the Institute for Advanced Study. He became an American citizen in 1940 but retained his Swiss citizenship.

In his later years, Einstein continued to work on his scientific research and became increasingly involved in political activism. He was a vocal critic of McCarthyism and the nuclear arms race during the Cold War era.

Einstein passed away on April 18, 1955, at the age of 76, leaving behind a legacy that transcended his scientific achievements. He remains one of the most iconic and influential figures of the 20th century, celebrated not only for his brilliance but also for his humanity and moral integrity.

Beyond his scientific achievements, Einstein became a symbol of intellectualism, humanism, and pacifism. He was an outspoken advocate for civil rights, peace, and democracy, using his platform to address issues such as racism and anti-Semitism. He famously warned of the dangers of nuclear weapons and called for international cooperation to prevent catastrophic conflict.

Einstein's fame transcended the scientific community, making him one of the most recognizable figures of the 20th century. His iconic image, with his wild hair and distinctive moustache, is instantly recognizable. He became a cultural icon, referenced in countless works of literature, art, and popular culture.

While Einstein's contributions were undoubtedly profound, it's important to remember that he was a human being, with flaws and limitations like anyone else. He experienced personal struggles and professional setbacks throughout his life. However, his unparalleled intellect, creativity, and moral conviction continue to inspire generations of scientists, thinkers, and activists around the world. So, while describing him as a "mortal god on earth" might be an exaggeration, it reflects the reverence and admiration many hold for his remarkable legacy.

Widely regarded as one of the greatest physicists of all time, Albert Einstein revolutionized our understanding of the universe with his theories of relativity and contributions to quantum mechanics. Beyond his scientific genius, Einstein was an outspoken advocate for peace, civil rights, and humanitarian causes, using his platform to promote social justice and international cooperation.

One particular story that is often recounted about Albert Einstein involves his response to a letter from a young girl named Phyllis Wright in 1936. Phyllis, a sixth-grader from San Francisco, wrote to Einstein asking whether scientists prayed and if so, what they prayed for. Einstein's reply to Phyllis's letter is both touching and profound. He expressed his admiration for her curiosity and thoughtful question. In his response, Einstein explained that while scientists, like everyone else, experience a sense of wonder and awe at the beauty and harmony of the universe, their "prayer" is in the form of trying to understand the laws of nature. He wrote:

"Scientific research is based on the idea that everything that takes place is determined by laws of nature, and therefore this holds for the actions of people. For this reason, a scientist will hardly be inclined to believe that events could be influenced by a prayer, i.e., by a wish addressed to a supernatural Being."

However, he acknowledged the importance of a spirit of reverence and humility in scientific inquiry:

"Nevertheless, everyone who is seriously involved in the pursuit of science becomes convinced that a spirit is manifest in the laws of the Universe—a spirit vastly superior to that of man, and one in the face of which we with our modest powers must feel humble."

Einstein's response highlights his deep respect for the mysteries of the universe and the humility with which he approached his own scientific inquiries. It also reflects his belief in the unity and interconnectedness of all things, a theme that permeates much of his philosophical and scientific thought.

This story resounds with many because it humanizes Einstein, showing his willingness to engage with questions beyond the field of physics and to connect with young minds who were curious about the world around them. It also showcases his ability to articulate complex ideas in a clear and accessible manner, making him not only a brilliant scientist but also a thoughtful and compassionate individual.

Malala Yousafzai

A fearless advocate for girls' education and human rights, Malala Yousafzai disobeyed the Taliban in her native Pakistan and survived a targeted assassination attempt at the age of 15. Since then, she has become an international symbol of courage , speaking out on behalf of millions of marginalized children and inspiring change through her activism and advocacy.

Malala Yousafzai's story is one of remarkable courage, resilience, and advocacy for education and girls' rights. Born on July 12, 1997, in Mingora, Pakistan, Malala grew up in the Swat Valley, where her father, Ziauddin Yousafzai, ran a chain of schools. Malala's childhood was marked by her father's passion for education and her own love of learning. She attended the Khushal Public School in Mingora, where she excelled academically and developed a deep commitment to education. However, the tranquillity of Malala's childhood was shattered in 2007 when the Taliban gained control of the Swat Valley. Under Taliban rule, girls were banned from attending school, and women faced severe restrictions on their freedom and rights. Despite the dangers, Malala continued to attend school and speak out against the Taliban's oppressive policies.

In early 2009, Malala began anonymously blogging for the BBC Urdu under the pseudonym Gul Makai, documenting her experiences living under Taliban rule and advocating for girls' education. Her bravery and outspokenness gathered international attention and admiration.

Tragically, Malala's activism made her a target for the Taliban. On October 9, 2012, as she was returning home from school, a gunman boarded her school bus and shot her in the head at point-blank range. The attack left Malala critically injured, and she was airlifted to Birmingham, England, for emergency medical treatment.

Miraculously, Malala survived the assassination attempt and underwent multiple surgeries and intensive rehabilitation. Her remarkable recovery captured the world's attention and inspired an outpouring of support and solidarity.

Following her recovery, Malala emerged as a global advocate for girls' education and human rights. In 2013, she co-founded the Malala Fund, a non-profit organization dedicated to ensuring every girl has access to 12 years of free, safe, and quality education. She also became the youngest-ever recipient of the Nobel Peace Prize in 2014, at the age of 17, in recognition of her courageous advocacy for girls' education.

Malala's story has since become a symbol of hope and resilience, inspiring millions of people around the world to stand up for justice, equality, and the power of education. Despite facing unimaginable adversity, Malala remains steadfast in her commitment to creating a better world for all children, regardless of their gender or background.

Fred Rogers: Wont you be my Neighbor?

Fred Rogers, known to millions as "Mister Rogers," was a beloved television personality who profoundly influenced generations of children through his ground-breaking show, "Mister Rogers' Neighbourhood." Born on March 20, 1928, in Latrobe, Pennsylvania, Fred Rogers had a passion for music and puppetry from a young age.

After graduating from college, Rogers pursued a career in television, eventually joining the Canadian Broadcasting Corporation (CBC) in the early 1960s. It was during his time at CBC that he developed the concept for "Mister Rogers' Neighbourhood," a children's program focused on fostering social and emotional development in young viewers. The show premiered in 1968 and quickly became a cultural phenomenon. Set in the fictional Neighbourhood of Make-Believe, "Mister Rogers' Neighbourhood" used puppets, music, and simple sets to explore complex themes such as kindness, empathy, and self-esteem. Each episode began with Rogers entering his home, singing his iconic theme song, "Won't You Be My Neighbor?" and changing into his trademark cardigan and sneakers.

One of the most distinctive aspects of "Mister Rogers' Neighbourhood" was Rogers' gentle and sympathetic behaviour. He spoke directly to his young viewers, addressing them as "neighbours," and encouraged them to express their feelings and emotions. His messages of acceptance, understanding, and love resonated deeply with children and parents alike. Throughout its run, "Mister Rogers' Neighbourhood" tackled important topics such as divorce, death, and disabilities with honesty and sensitivity. Rogers was committed to providing children with a safe and nurturing space where they could learn about the world around them and develop a sense of self-worth.

Beyond his television work, Rogers was also a passionate advocate for public broadcasting and children's education. He testified before Congress on multiple occasions, advocating for increased funding for educational programming and the importance of nurturing children's emotional well-being.

Fred Rogers' impact extended far beyond the field of television. He published numerous books, received countless awards and honours, and continued to inspire others through his public speaking engagements and appearances. His legacy lives on through the continued influence of "Mister Rogers' Neighbourhood" and the enduring lessons of kindness and compassion that he imparted to millions of viewers.

Fred Rogers passed away on February 27, 2003, but his timeless message of love and acceptance continues to resonate with audiences of all ages. He remains a beloved and iconic figure, fondly remembered as a true champion of children's rights and a beacon of hope and positivity in an often-chaotic world.

Martin Luther King:
The Champion of Nonviolent Change and Civil Rights

" His letter From Birmingham Jail"

Martin Luther King Jr. was a key figure in American history, known for his leadership in the Civil Rights Movement and his advocacy for nonviolent resistance against racial segregation and discrimination. Born on January 15, 1929, in Atlanta, Georgia, Martin Luther King Jr. was the second child of Michael King Sr., a pastor, and Alberta Williams King, a former schoolteacher. An exceptional student, he skipped grades and entered Morehouse College at 15, graduating with a degree in sociology in 1948. He then attended Crozer Theological Seminary, where he became president of his mostly white senior class, and earned his doctorate in systematic theology from Boston University in 1955.

King first gained national attention as a leader of the Montgomery Bus Boycott in 1955, sparked by Rosa Parks' arrest. His leadership in the year-long boycott, which led to the desegregation of the Montgomery bus system, propelled him to the forefront of the civil rights movement. In 1957, he co-founded the Southern Christian Leadership Conference (SCLC) to harness the power of black churches for civil rights reform.

As SCLC president, King led nonviolent demonstrations in Birmingham, Alabama, in 1963, which were met with violent police responses. The brutality shocked the nation and increased support for civil rights. During the Birmingham campaign, King was arrested and wrote his famous "Letter from Birmingham Jail," advocating for nonviolent resistance and the moral duty to disobey unjust laws.

On August 28, 1963, Martin Luther King Jr. delivered his iconic "I Have a Dream" speech during the March on Washington for Jobs and Freedom, addressing over 250,000 people and calling for an end to racism and the attainment of civil and economic rights. This moment is considered a pivotal point in the civil rights movement. In 1964, King was awarded the Nobel Peace Prize at the age of 35, making him the youngest recipient at that time.

In 1965, King organized and led the Selma to Montgomery marches to advocate for African American voting rights. The violent response to these marches, known as "Bloody Sunday," led to widespread outrage and the passage of the Voting Rights Act of 1965. Later, King focused on economic justice and poverty, organizing the Poor People's Campaign to address these issues.

Martin Luther King Jr. was assassinated on April 4, 1968, in Memphis, Tennessee, where he was supporting striking sanitation workers. His death led to riots across the United States and a national period of mourning. King's efforts were crucial in the passage of the Civil Rights Act of 1964 and the Voting Rights Act of 1965, leaving a lasting legacy in the fight for justice and equality.

He is remembered as a symbol of the fight for justice and equality, and his life and work have inspired countless individuals and movements worldwide. In 1983, the U.S. Congress established Martin Luther King Jr. Day as a national holiday, observed on the third Monday in January, to honour his legacy. King's advocacy for nonviolence, his eloquent speeches, and his unwavering commitment to justice have left an indelible mark on American history and continue to inspire social justice movements around the world.

The Story of the Montgomery Bus Boycott

In December 1955, Rosa Parks, an African American woman, was arrested in Montgomery, Alabama, for refusing to give up her bus seat to a white passenger. This incident sparked outrage in the black community and led to the Montgomery Bus Boycott. Martin Luther King Jr., then a young priest at Dexter Avenue Baptist Church, was chosen to lead the boycott due to his expression and strong moral presence.

King and other civil rights leaders organized the black community to refuse to ride the city buses. The boycott lasted for 381 days, during which African Americans walked, carpooled, and found other means of transportation despite facing harassment and violence. King's home was bombed, and he was arrested, but he remained steadfast in his commitment to nonviolent resistance.

The boycott ultimately led to a Supreme Court ruling that declared segregation on public buses unconstitutional. This victory was a monumental step in the civil rights movement and established King as a prominent leader in the fight for racial equality. His leadership during the boycott demonstrated the power of collective action and nonviolent protest, inspiring future movements and solidifying his legacy as a champion of justice.

Eleanor Roosevelt
Champion of Human Rights and Social Justice

Eleanor Roosevelt was a remarkable figure in American history, known for her tireless work as a humanitarian, diplomat, and advocate for civil rights. Born on October 11, 1884, in New York City, Eleanor came from a prominent family, being the niece of President Theodore Roosevelt. Her early life was marked by personal tragedy, losing both parents by the age of ten. Despite these hardships, she grew into a compassionate and determined individual.

Eleanor married Franklin D. Roosevelt, her fifth cousin. As Franklin pursued a career in politics, culminating in his election as the 32nd President of the United States, Eleanor redefined the role of the First Lady. She used her position to champion causes she believed in, breaking away from the traditionally ceremonial duties associated with the role. During Franklin's presidency, Eleanor became his eyes and ears, traveling extensively across the country to observe and report on the living conditions of ordinary Americans during the Great Depression.

One of Eleanor's significant contributions to humanity was her work with the United Nations. After Franklin's death in 1945, she was appointed as a delegate to the newly formed United Nations General Assembly by President Harry Truman. In this capacity, she chaired the committee that drafted the Universal Declaration of Human Rights, adopted in 1948. This landmark document set forth fundamental human rights to be universally protected and remains a cornerstone of international human rights law.

Eleanor Roosevelt was also a vocal advocate for civil rights. She supported anti-lynching legislation, championed the rights of African Americans and women, and fought against racial segregation. She resigned from the Daughters of the American Revolution (DAR) when they refused to allow African American singer Marian Anderson to perform at Constitution Hall, instead helping to arrange for Anderson's historic concert at the Lincoln Memorial.

Beyond her political work, Eleanor was a prolific writer and speaker. She authored a daily newspaper column, "My Day," from 1935 to 1962, where she addressed social issues and shared her views on a wide range of topics. Her speeches and writings inspired many to engage in public service and to fight for social justice.

Eleanor Roosevelt's legacy is one of profound impact on the fight for human rights, social justice, and equality. Her dedication to improving the lives of the disenfranchised and her role in shaping international human rights continue to influence and inspire activists and leaders around the world.

Abdul Sattar Edhi

Abdul Sattar Edhi was a Pakistani philanthropist, social activist, and humanitarian known for founding and leading the Edhi Foundation, one of the largest and most effective charitable organizations in Pakistan.

Abdul Sattar Edhi, born on February 28, 1928, in Bantva, Gujarat, British India, was profoundly influenced by his mother's compassion for the less fortunate. After moving to Karachi, Pakistan, post-partition in 1947, he was struck by the pervasive poverty. In 1951, starting with a small pharmacy, he laid the foundation of the Edhi Foundation, which grew to include free hospitals, clinics, maternity homes, orphanages, and shelters for the homeless. Notably, he established a nationwide ambulance service, the largest in Pakistan.

The Edhi Foundation also operated the "jhoola" project, where cradles were placed outside Edhi centers for people to leave unwanted babies safely, reducing the number of abandoned infants. Despite managing a large charitable network, Edhi lived in a modest house and owned very few personal possessions, dedicating his life to serving humanity and often working long hours and responding personally to emergencies. His commitment to neutrality and impartiality meant that he helped people of all religions, ethnicities, and backgrounds, earning widespread respect and admiration. Although he faced bureaucratic hurdles, political pressure, and occasional threats due to his non-discriminatory approach to charity, his unwavering dedication to humanitarianism earned him numerous national and international awards, including the Ramon Magsaysay Award for Public Service in 1986.

Despite these honours, Edhi remained humble, often attributing his success to the collective efforts of his volunteers and supporters. Abdul Sattar Edhi passed away on July 8, 2016, at the age of 88, and his death was mourned across Pakistan and the world. His legacy lives on through the Edhi Foundation, which continues to provide critical services to millions of people. Edhi's work had a profound impact on Pakistan and beyond, demonstrating that one person, with a vision and unwavering determination, could create massive positive change in society. His emphasis on compassion, simplicity, and selflessness set a powerful example for future generations, and he is remembered as a beacon of hope, a guardian of the destitute, and a symbol of humanity's potential for goodness.

7. PIONEERS OF SOCIAL TRANSFORMATIOJN

VINOBA BHAVE

Vinoba Bhave was a prominent Indian freedom fighter and social reformer, best known for his Bhoodan (land gift) Movement. Born on September 11, 1895, in Maharashtra, India, Vinoba dedicated his life to promoting nonviolence, social justice, and land reform.

His journey towards becoming a prominent figure in India's independence movement began during his early years. Influenced by Mahatma Gandhi, Vinoba joined the nonviolent struggle for Indian independence and became one of Gandhi's closest disciples. He participated actively in various freedom movements, including the Salt Satyagraha (Salt March) of 1930.

Vinoba's commitment to nonviolence and social justice extended beyond India's struggle for independence. After India gained independence in 1947, he focused his efforts on addressing the issues of poverty, inequality, and landlessness that persisted in rural India.

The Bhoodan Movement, initiated by Vinoba in 1951, was a significant aspect of his work. In this movement, he walked from village to village, asking wealthy landowners to voluntarily donate a portion of their land to landless peasants. Vinoba believed in the power of voluntary land redistribution as a means to address the unequal distribution of land and alleviate poverty in rural areas. His persuasive abilities and moral authority inspired many landowners to contribute to the cause, leading to the redistribution of millions of acres of land.

The success of the Bhoodan Movement led to the establishment of the Gramdan (village gift) Movement, which aimed at creating self-sustaining and self-governing village communities. Through these movements, Vinoba sought to empower rural communities, promote economic self-sufficiency, and foster a sense of collective responsibility and solidarity.

Vinoba's philosophy was deeply rooted in Gandhian principles of nonviolence, simplicity, and service to others. He believed in the inherent dignity and worth of every individual and advocated for social and economic justice for all members of society.

Throughout his life, Vinoba remained committed to his principles and continued his work for social reform and rural development. He received numerous awards and honours for his contributions, including the Ramon Magsaysay Award for Community Leadership in 1958.

Vinoba Bhave's legacy continues to inspire generations of social activists and reformers in India and around the world. His emphasis on nonviolence, voluntary action, and community empowerment serves as a timeless reminder of the power of individual conscience and collective action in the pursuit of social justice and human dignity.

ELA BHATT

Ela Bhatt was a remarkable Indian social activist and pioneer in the field of women's empowerment and labour rights. Born on September 7, 1933, in Ahmedabad, Gujarat, India, she dedicated her life to advocating for the rights of marginalized communities, particularly women and workers in the informal sector.

Bhatt's journey towards becoming a prominent social activist began during her early years. She was deeply influenced by the teachings of Mahatma Gandhi, particularly his principles of nonviolence and social justice. After earning a degree in law from the Sir L.A. Shah Law College in Ahmedabad, Bhatt joined the legal profession. However, her passion for social justice and empowerment led her to leave her legal practice and pursue activism full-time.

In 1972, she founded the Self-Employed Women's Association (SEWA) to support women in the informal sector, providing access to financial services, healthcare, childcare, and skills training. Under her leadership, SEWA became a powerful force for social change, advocating for policy reforms and legal protections for informal workers. Bhatt's innovative approach to grassroots organizing and her emphasis on collective action and solidarity resonated with women across India, leading to SEWA's expansion into various states and sectors.

One of Bhatt's most significant contributions was her pioneering work in microfinance and cooperative banking.

Recognizing the financial exclusion faced by women in the informal sector, she established SEWA Bank in 1974, India's first women's cooperative bank. SEWA Bank provided low-interest loans and financial services tailored to the needs of women, enabling them to start and expand their businesses and improve their economic well-being.

There are several anecdotes and stories associated with Ela Bhatt that illustrate her dedication to social justice and empowerment. One particularly famous story involves the founding of the Self-Employed Women's Association (SEWA).

Legend has it that the idea for SEWA was born during a visit by Ela Bhatt to a small village in Gujarat. While speaking with the women in the village, she learned about their struggles as self-employed workers in the informal sector. These women faced numerous challenges, including low wages, lack of access to financial services, and little to no social protection. Moved by their plight, Ela Bhatt realized the need for an organization that would advocate for the rights and interests of such women. She envisioned a platform where these women could come together, support each other, and collectively address the issues they faced.

With this vision in mind, Ela Bhatt founded SEWA in 1972. The organization began as a small women's collective in Ahmedabad but quickly expanded across Gujarat and beyond. SEWA pioneered approaches to women's empowerment, including microfinance, skills training, and policy advocacy. This story reflects Bhatt's empathy and commitment to marginalized communities, highlighting her belief in collective action to drive positive change.

Throughout her career, Bhatt promoted gender equality, economic justice, and human rights. She advocated for the rights of women workers, fought against exploitative practices, and championed fair wages. Her efforts garnered international recognition, including the Ramon Magsaysay Award in 1977 and the Padma Bhushan in 1986.

Ela Bhatt's legacy continues to inspire social activists and feminists worldwide. Her advocacy for marginalized communities has significantly impacted India's social landscape, shaping inclusive and empowering policies. She passed away on November 20, 2022, but her spirit and legacy live on through the lives she touched and the movements she inspired.

JADAV PAYENG

Jadav Payeng, also known as the "Forest Man of India," is an environmental activist and forestry worker from the north eastern state of Assam. His remarkable story is one of unwavering dedication to reforestation and environmental conservation.

Born in 1963 on Majuli, a river island in the Brahmaputra River, Payeng grew up surrounded by the natural beauty of Assam's lush landscapes. In 1979, when he was just 16 years old, Payeng witnessed a devastating sight: large-scale erosion had left a barren sandbar on the river island, devoid of any vegetation and wildlife. This event deeply affected him, igniting a passion to restore the island's ecosystem.

Motivated by a desire to combat erosion and protect the environment, Payeng decided to take action. Armed with determination and a strong work ethic, he began planting saplings on the barren sandbar. Despite facing scepticism and criticism from locals and authorities, Payeng remained undeterred in his mission.

For several years, Payeng devoted himself to nurturing the newly planted trees, often single-handedly tending to them with basic tools and buckets of water. His efforts gradually transformed the once-barren sandbar into a thriving forest ecosystem. Over time, the area became home to a diverse range of flora and fauna, including trees, shrubs, grasses, birds, mammals, and even reptiles.

Payeng's forest, now known as the Molai Forest or Molai Woods, spans over 1,360 acres and is considered one of the largest man-made forests in the world. It serves as a testament to the power of individual initiative and environmental stewardship.

The Molai Forest has attracted widespread attention and acclaim, earning Payeng recognition as a conservation hero both in India and internationally. His story has been documented in numerous articles, films, and documentaries, inspiring people around the globe to take action to protect the environment.

In addition to his work as a forest conservationist, Payeng has been involved in various environmental initiatives, including campaigns to raise awareness about deforestation, climate change, and wildlife conservation. He continues to advocate for sustainable development practices and the preservation of natural habitats.

Jadav Payeng's story exemplifies the profound impact that one person can have on the environment through dedication, perseverance, and a deep connection to the land. His legacy serves as a reminder of the importance of individual action in addressing global environmental challenges and protecting the planet for future generations.

Anand Kumar

Anand Kumar is an Indian mathematician and educator who gained widespread recognition for his pioneering work in providing quality mathematics education to underprivileged students. Born on January 1, 1973, in Patna, Bihar, India, his story is one of resilience, passion for education, and a relentless commitment to social change.

Growing up in a modest household in Patna, Kumar showed an early aptitude for mathematics. Despite facing financial constraints, he pursued his passion for learning and completed his education at the prestigious Cambridge University in England. However, upon returning to India, he was confronted with the harsh reality of educational inequality and the lack of opportunities for talented students from disadvantaged backgrounds.

Determined to make a difference, Kumar founded the Super 30 program in 2002. The program aimed to provide free coaching and support to 30 underprivileged students from economically backward communities to help them prepare for the highly competitive Indian Institutes of Technology Joint Entrance Examination (IIT-JEE).

What set Super 30 apart was Kumar's innovative approach to teaching and mentorship. He personally selected students from impoverished backgrounds who demonstrated exceptional mathematical talent but lacked the resources to afford coaching classes. Kumar and his team provided these students with free lodging, food, study materials, and intensive coaching for the duration of the program.

Despite facing numerous challenges, including financial constraints and skepticism from critics, Kumar's Super 30 program achieved remarkable success. Year after year, a significant number of his students, often from the most marginalized sections of society, secured admission to prestigious Indian Institutes of Technology (IITs), some of the most esteemed engineering institutions in India.

The success of Super 30 garnered widespread attention and awards, both nationally and internationally. Kumar's story was featured in documentaries, books, and media outlets, inspiring millions of people around the world with its message of hope, determination, and the transformative power of education.

Beyond Super 30, Kumar has been involved in various initiatives aimed at promoting mathematics education and empowering disadvantaged youth. He continues to advocate for educational reform and equal access to quality education for all children, regardless of their social background.

Anand Kumar's story serves as a shining example of the transformative impact that one individual can have on the lives of others through education and empowerment. His dedication to nurturing talent, breaking barriers, and challenging the status quo has earned him admiration and respect as an example of hope and inspiration for generations to come.

Sindhutai Sapkal

Sindhutai Sapkal, often referred to as the "Mother of Orphans," was born on November 14, 1948, in Pimpri Meghe, Wardha district, Maharashtra. Growing up in a family of cattle grazers, she faced severe poverty from a young age. Despite her desire to study, she was forced to quit school after the fourth grade due to her family's financial situation and societal norms. At the age of 12, she was married to Shrihari Sapkal, a man 20 years her senior, and moved to Navargaon village in Wardha.

Sindhutai's marital life was marked by extreme hardships. Her husband was abusive and their financial situation dire. When she was 20 years old and nine months pregnant, her husband abandoned her following false accusations of infidelity. Homeless and destitute, Sindhutai gave birth to her daughter, Mamta, in a cowshed. She turned to begging to survive, often sleeping at railway stations and begging for food on streets and platforms.

Despite her dire circumstances, Sindhutai found a new purpose in life when she saw orphaned and abandoned children living in hopeless conditions. She resolved to take care of these children, identifying with their plight. Initially, she started by begging more vigorously, not for herself, but for the children she began to adopt and care for. Over time, her efforts drew attention, and people began to support her mission.

With sheer determination and relentless effort, Sindhutai founded her first orphanage, "Sanmati Bal Niketan," in Hadapsar, Pune. Her journey was filled with challenges, including severe financial constraints, but she never wavered in her commitment. Over the years, she established multiple orphanages across Maharashtra. By the time of her passing, she had nurtured and provided a home to over 1,500 orphaned and abandoned children. Many of these children went on to become doctors, engineers, and other professionals, contributing positively to society. Sindhutai's work earned her numerous honours and recognition. She received over 750 awards for her social service, including the Padma Shri in 2021, one of India's highest civilian honours. Her life and work have been documented in various media, including the acclaimed Marathi biographical film "Mee Sindhutai Sapkal," which brought her story to a wider audience.

In addition to her work with orphans, Sindhutai was a powerful advocate for the rights of women and the marginalized. She gave numerous speeches and lectures, sharing her story and encouraging others to contribute to social welfare. Her philosophy centered on the idea that true happiness and fulfillment come from serving others, particularly those in need.

Sindhutai passed away on January 4, 2022, due to cardiac arrest. However, her legacy continues through the institutions she established and the countless lives she touched. Her story remains a powerful testament to the impact one determined individual can have on society, transforming lives through sheer willpower, compassion, and relentless dedication.

Dr. Devi Prasad Shetty

Dr. Devi Prasad Shetty, born in 1953, is a renowned Indian cardiac surgeon and entrepreneur whose journey is as fascinating as it is inspiring. His story is one of passion, innovation, and a relentless pursuit of making healthcare accessible to all.

Growing up in a small village in Karnataka, India, Shetty's early life was far removed from the world of medicine and surgery. However, his inborn curiosity and drive led him to pursue a career in medicine. After completing his medical education, Shetty's journey took him to England, where he trained and honed his skills as a cardiac surgeon.

Upon returning to India, Shetty was struck by the glaring disparities in healthcare access and affordability. Determined to make a difference, he founded Narayana Hrudayalaya (now known as Narayana Health), a multi-specialty hospital chain, in Bangalore in 2001. His vision was clear: to provide world-class healthcare at a fraction of the cost.

Under Shetty's leadership, Narayana Health revolutionized the healthcare landscape in India. Through innovative practices and economies of scale, the hospital chain was able to offer high-quality medical services at prices significantly lower than those of its counterparts. Shetty's approach to healthcare delivery focused on efficiency, technology adoption, and sympathetic care.

One of the most remarkable aspects of Shetty's work is his commitment to reaching the underserved population. Recognizing the importance of preventive care and early intervention, he launched numerous outreach programs and initiatives aimed at providing healthcare to remote and rural areas. His efforts have touched the lives of millions, bringing hope and healing to those who previously had little access to medical services.

Beyond his work with Narayana Health, Shetty is also known for his contributions to medical research and education. He has been involved in pioneering techniques in cardiac surgery, including low-cost heart surgeries and innovative surgical methods. Additionally, he has been instrumental in training the next generation of healthcare professionals, ensuring that his legacy extends far beyond his own achievements.

Throughout his career, Shetty has garnered widespread recognition and tributes for his contributions to healthcare. He has received numerous awards and honours, including the Padma Bhushan, one of India's highest civilian awards, for his exceptional service to the nation. Dr. Devi Prasad Shetty's story is a testament to the power of one individual's vision to transform an entire industry. Through his passion, dedication, and unwavering commitment to serving others, he has not only revolutionized healthcare in India but has also inspired countless others to follow in his footsteps.

One unique and touching story associated with Dr. Devi Prasad Shetty revolves around his commitment to providing healthcare to those who cannot afford it, even in the face of financial challenges.

In 2012, a young girl named Roona Begum captured the world's attention when photographs of her went viral. Roona was born in a remote village in Tripura, India, with an extremely rare condition called hydrocephalus, which caused her head to swell to an enormous size due to the accumulation of cerebrospinal fluid.

Roona's family, living in poverty, struggled to afford her medical treatment. The images of Roona's swollen head sparked a global outpouring of sympathy and support, with people from around the world donating money to help cover her medical expenses.

Dr. Devi Prasad Shetty, hearing about Roona's plight, was deeply moved and offered to provide her with free medical treatment at Narayana Health in Bangalore. Despite the complexities of Roona's condition and the high costs associated with her treatment, Shetty and his team were determined to help her.

Roona underwent multiple surgeries over the course of several months to drain the excess fluid from her brain and reduce the size of her head. Despite the challenges, Shetty and his team worked tirelessly to ensure the best possible outcome for Roona.

The story of Roona Begum touched the hearts of millions around the world, and Dr. Devi Prasad Shetty's compassionate response highlighted his unwavering commitment to providing healthcare to those in need, regardless of their financial circumstances.

Through his actions, Shetty not only saved Roona's life but also demonstrated the power of compassion and empathy in healthcare. The story of Roona Begum serves as a poignant reminder of the impact that one individual, driven by a sense of duty and compassion, can have on the lives of others.

Dr. M.S. Swaminathan

Dr. Monkombu Sambasivan Swaminathan, born on August 7, 1925, in Kumbakonam, Tamil Nadu, was a distinguished Indian agricultural scientist and geneticist renowned for his pivotal role in sustainable farming and food security. His story is one of tireless dedication to improving the lives of farmers and combating hunger through innovation and scientific research.

Rooted in a family with a deep agricultural background, Swaminathan's passion for farming blossomed early. He earned his Bachelor of Science in agriculture from the University of Madras, followed by a Master's in genetics and plant breeding from the Indian Agricultural Research Institute. Furthering his education, he pursued a Ph.D. in plant genetics at the University of Wisconsin-Madison, where exposure to advanced research profoundly influenced his work.

Upon returning to India, Swaminathan held esteemed positions in government and research institutions, including the Indian Agricultural Research Institute and the Indian Council of Agricultural Research. He played a crucial role in the Green Revolution by introducing high-yielding wheat and rice varieties, transforming India into a self-sufficient agricultural nation.

Swaminathan's most significant contributions came in the area of agricultural innovation and technology transfer. He played a pivotal role in introducing high-yielding varieties of wheat and rice to India during the Green Revolution of the 1960s and 1970s. These new crop varieties, coupled with improved irrigation and farming techniques, helped transform India from a food-deficit nation to a self-sufficient agricultural powerhouse.

Beyond his work with high-yielding crops, Swaminathan also advocated for sustainable farming practices and biodiversity conservation. He emphasized the importance of preserving traditional knowledge and crop diversity to ensure long-term food security and environmental sustainability.

Swaminathan's impact extended beyond India's borders. He was actively involved in international agricultural development initiatives and served as the Director General of the International Rice Research Institute (IRRI) in the Philippines from 1982 to 1988.

Throughout his career, Swaminathan received numerous awards and honours for his contributions to agriculture and rural development. He was awarded the Padma Bhushan and the Padma Vibhushan, two of India's highest civilian honours, for his exceptional service to the nation. Even in his later years, Swaminathan remained actively engaged in promoting sustainable agriculture and advocating for the welfare of farmers. He continued to inspire generations of agricultural scientists and policymakers through his research, writing, and public speaking.

Dr. M.S. Swaminathan's legacy as the "Father of the Green Revolution in India" and a global leader in agricultural science continues to resonate today. His visionary leadership, innovative research, and unwavering commitment to feeding the world have left an indelible mark on the history of agriculture and human development.

One particularly fascinating and lesser-known story associated with Dr. M.S. Swaminathan revolves around his efforts to preserve and promote indigenous rice varieties in India.

In the 1980s, Swaminathan grew alarmed by the loss of traditional rice varieties in India due to the Green Revolution's focus on high-yielding hybrids. These ancient varieties, cultivated for generations, were being replaced by monoculture crops, resulting in a significant loss of biodiversity and genetic resources. Understanding the critical importance of these indigenous varieties for their genetic diversity and resilience, Swaminathan led a campaign to collect, conserve, and document hundreds of rice types from across India. He collaborated with local farmers, agricultural scientists, and grassroots organizations to establish community seed banks and conservation programs, ensuring the long-term viability of these traditional seeds.

Swaminathan's vision extended beyond just conservation. He aimed to rekindle interest in these rice varieties and encouraged their cultivation among farmers. He recognized their potential to enhance sustainable agriculture and food security and promoted their reintroduction into fields.

A key element of Swaminathan's approach was participatory research and farmer empowerment. By involving farmers in the conservation and evaluation process, he leveraged their traditional knowledge and expertise, thereby preserving India's rich agricultural heritage and fostering sustainable farming practices. Through his efforts, Swaminathan not only helped preserve India's rich agricultural heritage but also contributed to the revitalization of rural communities and sustainable farming practices. By promoting the cultivation of indigenous rice varieties, he empowered farmers to diversify their crops, enhance resilience to climate change, and improve food security.

Today, Swaminathan's work in conserving indigenous rice varieties serves as a valuable example of the importance of preserving agricultural biodiversity and traditional knowledge. His efforts have inspired similar initiatives around the world and underscore the critical role of genetic diversity in ensuring the future sustainability of agriculture.

Kailash Satyarthi

Kailash Satyarthi, born on January 11, 1954, in Vidisha, Madhya Pradesh, India, is a Nobel Peace Prize winner known for his tireless advocacy and activism against child labour and for children's rights. His story is one of courage, compassion, and unwavering dedication to the most vulnerable members of society.

Satyarthi's journey began in India, where he witnessed first-hand the harsh realities faced by millions of children trapped in exploitative labour conditions. Moved by their suffering and inspired by Mahatma Gandhi's principles of non-violence and social justice, Satyarthi dedicated his life to fighting for the rights of these children.

After completing his education in engineering, Satyarthi abandoned a promising career to pursue his passion for social justice. He founded Bachpan Bachao Andolan (Save the Childhood Movement) in 1980, a grassroots organization aimed at rescuing and rehabilitating child laborers and advocating for policy changes to address the root causes of child exploitation.

One of Satyarthi's most notable tactics is his direct-action approach to rescue children from bonded labour, trafficking, and other forms of exploitation. He and his team conduct daring raids on factories, workshops, and other places where children are forced to work, often risking their own safety to liberate these young victims.

But Satyarthi's work doesn't stop at rescue operations. He also focuses on the rehabilitation and education of rescued children, providing them with access to schooling, vocational training, and psychological support to help them rebuild their lives.

Satyarthi's activism extends beyond India's borders. He has been instrumental in advocating for international treaties and conventions to protect children's rights, including the United Nations Convention on the Rights of the Child and the International Labour Organization's Convention on the Worst Forms of Child Labour.

In 2014, Satyarthi's decades-long dedication to the cause of child rights was globally recognized when he was awarded the Nobel Peace Prize, jointly with Pakistani education activist Malala Yousafzai. The Nobel Committee honoured Satyarthi for his "struggle against the suppression of children and young people and for the right of all children to education."

Despite receiving such prestigious recognition, Satyarthi remains humble and committed to his mission. He continues to tirelessly advocate for children's rights, traveling the world to raise awareness about the plight of child laborers and mobilizing support for their cause.

Kailash Satyarthi's story serves as a powerful reminder of the impact that one individual can have in bringing about positive change in the world. His unwavering commitment to the welfare of children has inspired millions and continues to drive progress towards a world free from child labour and exploitation.

One remarkable and relatively lesser-known story associated with Kailash Satyarthi is his involvement in the rescue of child laborers from hazardous and exploitative conditions in carpet factories in India.

In the late 1990s, Satyarthi and his organization, ***Bachpan Bachao Andolan*** (BBA), received information about children being forced to work in carpet factories in Uttar Pradesh, India, under terrible conditions. These children, some as young as five or six years old, were subjected to long hours of work, physical abuse, and denied access to education and basic necessities.

Despite facing considerable resistance from factory owners and local authorities, Satyarthi and his team embarked on a daring rescue mission to liberate these children and bring them to safety. The rescue operation involved careful planning, undercover investigations, and coordination with law enforcement agencies.

One particularly memorable rescue operation took place in 1998 in the town of Mirzapur, Uttar Pradesh, known for its carpet industry. Satyarthi and his team, accompanied by police officers, raided several carpet factories where children were known to be working. Despite facing threats and pressure from factory owners and middlemen, they remained steadfast in their mission to rescue the children.

During the raid, Satyarthi personally confronted the wrongdoers and demanded the release of the child laborers. He used his negotiation skills and moral authority to persuade the factory owners to cooperate and hand over the children to the authorities.

The rescue operation was successful, and dozens of children were liberated from bonded labour and exploitation. Satyarthi and his team provided immediate assistance to the rescued children, including medical care, counselling, and reunification with their families where possible.

The Mirzapur rescue operation garnered widespread attention and shed light on the rampant problem of child labour in India's carpet industry. It also served as a catalyst for policy changes and increased enforcement efforts to combat child labour and protect the rights of vulnerable children.

This rare story exemplifies Kailash Satyarthi's courage, determination, and commitment to rescuing children from exploitation and providing them with a chance for a better future. His relentless efforts have not only saved countless lives but have also inspired global action to eradicate child labour and uphold the rights of children everywhere.

Jane Goodall

Jane Goodall, born on April 3, 1934, in London, England, is a pioneering primatologist, conservationist, and advocate for wildlife conservation and environmental sustainability. Her story is one of ground-breaking scientific discoveries, lifelong dedication to studying chimpanzees, and tireless efforts to protect the natural world.

Goodall's fascination with animals began at a young age, nurtured by her love of nature and the stories of Dr. Dolittle. Despite not having a formal university education, Goodall's passion for animals led her to pursue a career in primatology, the study of monkeys.

In 1957, at the age of 23, Goodall embarked on a remarkable journey to Tanzania (then Tanganyika) to study chimpanzees in their natural habitat. Armed with little more than a notebook and binoculars, she began her ground-breaking research at Gombe Stream National Park. Goodall's approach to studying chimpanzees was revolutionary. Unlike traditional scientists who observed animals from a distance, she immersed herself in the chimpanzees' world, spending hours quietly observing their behaviour, social interactions, and family dynamics.

One of Goodall's most significant discoveries came in 1960 when she observed a chimpanzee named David Greybeard using a stick to fish for termites—a behaviour previously thought to be exclusive to humans. This ground-breaking observation challenged long-held beliefs about the uniqueness of human behaviour and forever changed our understanding of the animal kingdom. Goodall's research at Gombe Stream National Park continued for several decades, yielding numerous ground-breaking insights into chimpanzee behaviour, communication, and social structure. Her meticulous observations laid the foundation for modern primatology and inspired generations of scientists to study animal behaviour in their natural habitats.

In addition to her scientific contributions, Goodall became a leading voice for conservation and environmental activism. She recognized the urgent need to protect chimpanzees and their habitats from deforestation, poaching, and habitat destruction. In 1977, Goodall founded the Jane Goodall Institute (JGI), a global non-profit organization dedicated to wildlife conservation, habitat protection, and community-cantered conservation initiatives. Through JGI's innovative programs, including the Roots & Shoots youth program, Goodall has empowered millions of people, especially young people, to take action on behalf of the environment and make a positive difference in their communities.

Goodall's advocacy work has taken her around the world, where she continues to inspire audiences with her message of hope, compassion, and environmental stewardship. She has authored numerous books, appeared in documentaries, and received countless awards and honours for her contributions to science and conservation. Jane Goodall's story is a testament to the power of passion, curiosity, and perseverance in the pursuit of knowledge and the protection of our planet's precious biodiversity. Her lifelong dedication to studying and protecting chimpanzees has not only expanded our understanding of the natural world but has also inspired millions to join her in the fight to preserve our shared home, Eart

8. HUMANITARIAN LEADERS

Desmond Tutu

A South African Anglican bishop and social rights activist known for his role in the fight against racial discrimination and his work for reconciliation in post-discrimination South Africa.

Desmond Tutu, born on October 7, 1931, in Klerksdorp, South Africa, is a prominent figure in the struggle against apartheid and a renowned advocate for peace, justice, and human rights. His story is one of courage, compassion, and unwavering commitment to fighting injustice and promoting reconciliation. Tutu grew up in South Africa during a time of systemic racial segregation and discrimination. Despite facing numerous obstacles and hardships due to his race, Tutu excelled academically and eventually pursued a career in the Anglican Church.

Ordained as a priest in 1960, Tutu became increasingly involved in the anti-racial movement, using his position to speak out against racial injustice and advocate for nonviolent resistance. His powerful sermons and impassioned speeches earned him a reputation as a fearless champion of human rights.

In 1975, Tutu was appointed the first black Dean of St. Mary's Cathedral in Johannesburg, where he continued to denounce racial discrimination and support victims of racial oppression. His outspoken activism drew the anger of the apartheid government, which subjected him to harassment, surveillance, and threats.

Despite the risks, Tutu remained steadfast in his commitment to justice and reconciliation. In 1984, he was awarded the Nobel Peace Prize for his peaceful efforts to end racial discrimination and promote social justice in South Africa. During the late 1980s, as General Secretary of the South African Council of Churches, Tutu played a critical role in garnering international support for economic sanctions and diplomatic pressure against the discriminatory regime, aiding in its downfall.

After Nelson Mandela became South Africa's first black president in 1994, Tutu chaired the Truth and Reconciliation Commission (TRC), which investigated human rights violations and promoted healing. His compassionate leadership emphasized forgiveness and reconciliation, despite facing criticism. Tutu's leadership of the TRC was characterized by his compassionate approach to justice, which emphasized the importance of forgiveness and reconciliation in the aftermath of trauma and violence. Despite facing criticism and controversy, Tutu remained resolute in his belief that forgiveness and understanding were essential for building a more just and peaceful society. Throughout his life, Desmond Tutu has been a tireless advocate for human rights, peace, and social justice, both in South Africa and around the world. His legacy as a moral leader and champion of reconciliation continues to inspire generations of activists and leaders in the ongoing struggle for equality and dignity for all.

One particularly touching story associated with Desmond Tutu is his role in the 1989 Christmas Eve Massacre in Sebokeng, South Africa, during the height of apartheid.

Sebokeng, near Johannesburg, was a hotspot of protests against racial discrimination and unfair government policies. On December 24, 1989, a peaceful protest turned tragic when police opened fire on the crowd, killing at least 40 people, many shot in the back as they fled. Deeply disturbed, Desmond Tutu rushed to offer comfort and support to the grieving families. Despite the personal risks, he confronted the authorities and demanded accountability for the massacre.

In the aftermath of the tragedy, Tutu played a crucial role in providing solace to the bereaved families and advocating for justice. He spoke out against the violence and called for an independent investigation into the incident, denouncing the brutality of the unfair regime and its disregard for human rights. Tutu's presence in Sebokeng during this dark time provided an example of hope and solidarity for the community, reaffirming his unwavering commitment to justice and reconciliation. His actions also drew international attention to the human rights abuses perpetrated by the government and underscored the urgent need for political reform and democratization in South Africa.

The Christmas Eve Massacre in Sebokeng serves as a stark reminder of the violence and oppression suffered by black South Africans under racialism and the courage of those who stood up against injustice. Desmond Tutu's courageous response to the tragedy exemplifies his moral leadership and unwavering dedication to the pursuit of justice and peace.

Aung San Suu Kyi

A Burmese politician and Nobel Peace Prize winner known for her nonviolent struggle for democracy and human rights in Myanmar. The story of Aung San Suu Kyi is one of courage, strength, and unwavering commitment to democracy and human rights in Myanmar (formerly Burma). Born on June 19, 1945, in Rangoon (now Yangon), Suu Kyi is the daughter of General Aung San, a key figure in Burma's struggle for independence from British colonial rule. Suu Kyi spent much of her early life abroad due to her father's diplomatic career, receiving her education in India, the United Kingdom, and the United States. She studied philosophy, politics, and economics at Oxford University, where she met her husband, Michael Aris, a scholar of Tibetan culture.

In 1988, Suu Kyi returned to Burma to care for her ailing mother, coinciding with widespread pro-democracy protests. She emerged as a leader, co-founding the National League for Democracy (NLD), advocating for nonviolent resistance and democratic reform. Her leadership made her a target for the military regime, and she was placed under house arrest in 1989, spending 15 years in confinement over the next two decades.

Suu Kyi's leadership and popularity quickly made her a target of the ruling military regime, which viewed her as a threat to their authority. In 1989, she was placed under house arrest without trial, where she would spend a total of 15 years over the next two decades, separated from her family and isolated from the outside world.

Despite her confinement, Suu Kyi remained steadfast in her commitment to the principles of democracy and nonviolence. She continued to advocate for political reform and human rights through her writings, speeches, and interviews, becoming an international symbol of resistance against oppression and dictatorship. In 1991, while still under house arrest, Suu Kyi was awarded the Nobel Peace Prize for her "non-violent struggle for democracy and human rights." The award brought global attention to her cause and galvanized support for the pro-democracy movement in Burma.

Suu Kyi's determination and moral leadership played a pivotal role in Burma's transition to democracy in the early 2010s. Following years of international pressure and domestic reform efforts, the military regime allowed multiparty elections in 2015, which the NLD won in a landslide victory. In a historic moment, Suu Kyi assumed the role of State Counsellor of Myanmar, a position created specifically for her since the constitution barred her from the presidency due to her foreign-born children. As State Counsellor, Suu Kyi became the de facto leader of Myanmar, overseeing the country's transition to civilian rule and implementing reforms aimed at strengthening democracy and promoting national reconciliation. However, Suu Kyi's tenure as State Counsellor has been marred by controversy, particularly regarding her response to the cruelty of the Rohingya Muslim minority in Rakhine State. Critics accuse her government of turning a blind eye to human rights abuses and ethnic cleansing perpetrated by the military against the Rohingya, a charge Suu Kyi vehemently denies.

In 2021, Suu Kyi's leadership was once again put to the test when the military staged a coup and seized power, alleging voter fraud in the 2020 general elections, which the NLD won by a landslide. Suu Kyi, along with other elected officials, was detained by the military, plunging Myanmar back into authoritarian rule and sparking widespread protests and civil unrest.

Despite facing numerous challenges and setbacks throughout her life, Aung San Suu Kyi remains a symbol of hope for the people of Myanmar and for democracy advocates around the world. Her unwavering dedication to the principles of democracy, human rights, and nonviolence continues to inspire millions, cementing her legacy as one of the most influential political figures of the 20th and 21st centuries.

One particularly notable story associated with Aung San Suu Kyi is her decision to return to Burma in 1988 to care for her ailing mother, despite the ongoing political turmoil and repressive atmosphere in the country.

In 1988, Burma was in the midst of a pro-democracy uprising against the military dictatorship that had ruled the country since 1962. Suu Kyi, who had been living abroad for many years, was settled in England with her husband and children, pursuing a quiet life as an academic and raising her family.

However, when Suu Kyi received news of her mother's declining health, she faced a difficult decision. Despite the risks posed by Burma's authoritarian regime and the uncertain political situation, Suu Kyi chose to return to her homeland to be with her mother in her final days.

Upon her return to Burma, Suu Kyi was immediately swept up in the increasing pro-democracy movement. Inspired by the courage and determination of the demonstrators, she began to speak out against the military regime and call for democratic reform.

Suu Kyi's decision to stay in Burma and join the pro-democracy movement was a turning point in her life and in the history of the country. Despite the personal risks and sacrifices involved, she chose to stand with her fellow citizens in their struggle for freedom and democracy. In the years that followed, Suu Kyi emerged as a key leader of the pro-democracy movement and a symbol of hope for the Burmese people. Her decision to return to Burma and take a stand against dictatorship demonstrated her deep commitment to the principles of democracy, human rights, and national reconciliation.

This story exemplifies Aung San Suu Kyi's courage, strenght, and unwavering dedication to the cause of democracy and freedom in Burma. It serves as a powerful reminder of the personal sacrifices she has made in her lifelong struggle for justice and human rights.

Elie Wiesel

Elie Wiesel was born in 1928 in Romania. When he was a teenager, he and his family were sent to a concentration camp during World War II because they were Jewish. Elie and his father survived terrible conditions in Auschwitz and Buchenwald, but his mother and sisters did not.

After the war, Elie moved to France and started writing about his experiences. His book "Night," which came out in 1956, tells the story of what he went through during the Holocaust. It became very famous and is now read all over the world to remember what happened.

Elie Wiesel didn't just write books; he became a leader in speaking out against hate and for human rights. He won the Nobel Peace Prize in 1986 for his work to make the world a better place. Throughout his life, he inspired people to stand up against injustice and to remember the lessons of history, so that such terrible things never happen again.

Elie Wiesel passed away in 2016, but his legacy lives on through his writings and his efforts to make the world more peaceful and fair for everyone. Elie Wiesel, like millions of others during the Holocaust, was sent to a concentration camp solely because he was Jewish. The Holocaust was a horrific period during World War II when Nazi Germany, led by Adolf Hitler, targeted Jewish people and others deemed undesirable by the regime. The Nazis believed in a dangerous ideology of racial superiority and sought to eliminate entire groups of people they considered inferior.

Elie Wiesel and his family were caught in this brutal system of discrimination and persecution. They were rounded up, separated from their community, and deported to concentration camps where they suffered unimaginable suffering, forced labour, starvation, and often death. The Holocaust remains one of history's darkest chapters, a stark reminder of the consequences of hatred, prejudice, and unchecked power. The Holocaust, also known as the Shoah in Hebrew, refers to the systematic, state-sponsored persecution and genocide of six million Jews by Nazi Germany and its collaborators during World War II. This genocide was carried out between 1941 and 1945 in German-occupied territories and across Nazi-occupied Europe.

The Nazis implemented their genocidal policies through methods such as forced labour, ghettos, deportations to concentration and extermination camps, and systematic murder through gas chambers, mass shootings, starvation, and other forms of brutality. The Holocaust represents one of the darkest periods in human history, where racial hatred and intolerance led to the annihilation of millions of innocent lives. It is essential to remember the Holocaust to honour the memories of its victims, to educate future generations about the consequences of unchecked hatred and discrimination, and to reaffirm a commitment to tolerance, respect for human dignity, and the prevention of genocide.

In his memoir "Night," Elie Wiesel vividly recounts his harrowing experiences as a teenager during the Holocaust. He describes the deportation of his family from their home in Sighet, Romania, to Auschwitz concentration camp, where he and his father faced extreme suffering, hunger, and cruelty at the hands of the Nazis. Wiesel depicts the gradual loss of his faith in God and humanity as he witnesses atrocities and the deaths of loved ones. "Night" is a powerful and haunting account that bears witness to the horrors of the Holocaust and the toughness of the human spirit in the face of unimaginable evil.

In the concentration camps, Elie Wiesel faced a relentless bombardment of atrocities that tested the limits of human stamina and shattered his faith in humanity. Forced into slave labour, he and other prisoners toiled under harsh conditions, facing starvation, exhaustion, and constant physical abuse from Nazi guards. The daily struggle for survival included meagre rations of food and water, inadequate shelter in overcrowded barracks, and exposure to disease.

Beyond the physical hardships, the camps were sites of profound dehumanization. Prisoners were stripped of their identities and subjected to humiliating treatment, such as being shaved, stripped naked, and tattooed with identification numbers. The Nazi regime's systematic dehumanization extended to cruel medical experiments, forced sterilizations, and the separation of families upon arrival.

The most chilling aspect of the camps was the routine selections, where Nazi officers decided who would live and who would die. Those deemed unfit for labour—often the elderly, sick, and young children—were sent to gas chambers for extermination. The horror continued with the disposal of bodies in crematoria, where the scale of mass murder became tragically apparent.

For Elie Wiesel, witnessing these atrocities shattered his innocence and deeply challenged his beliefs. He grappled with the loss of faith in God and questioned how such evil could exist in the world. His memoir "Night" serves not only as a personal account of survival but also as a touching testament to the lasting human spirit amidst unimaginable suffering and the imperative to remember and learn from history's darkest chapter, the Holocaust.

Elie Wiesel dedicated his life to humanitarian causes and advocacy for justice and human rights after surviving the Holocaust. Here are some of the key contributions he made for humanity:

Holocaust Remembrance: Wiesel became a prominent voice for Holocaust remembrance, ensuring that the atrocities committed during that period were not forgotten. His memoir "Night" became a seminal work in Holocaust literature, educating people around the world about the horrors of genocide.

Advocacy Against Genocide: Wiesel was a tireless advocate against genocide and crimes against humanity. He spoke out against atrocities in places like Bosnia, Darfur, and Rwanda, urging the international community to intervene and prevent such tragedies.

Peace and Reconciliation: Wiesel was a staunch advocate for peace and reconciliation among peoples and nations. He believed in dialogue and understanding as paths toward healing and preventing future conflicts.

Human Rights: Wiesel worked to promote human rights globally, advocating for the rights of oppressed peoples, including Palestinians and Kurds. He emphasized the importance of standing up against oppression and discrimination in all its forms.

Education: Wiesel was deeply committed to education as a means to combat ignorance and intolerance. He taught at Boston University for many years, inspiring countless students to engage critically with history and human rights issues.

Founding of Organizations: He co-founded the United States Holocaust Memorial Museum in Washington, D.C., and the Elie Wiesel Foundation for Humanity, which focused on combating indifference, intolerance, and injustice through education and dialogue.

Recognition and Awards: In 1986, Elie Wiesel was awarded the Nobel Peace Prize for his role in speaking out against oppression and injustice. This recognition highlighted his global impact and dedication to promoting peace and human dignity.

Elie Wiesel's life and work exemplify a lifelong commitment to speaking truth to power, advocating for those who cannot advocate for themselves, and striving to ensure that the lessons of history are learned and applied to create a better world for future generations.

Wangari Maathai:

Kenyan environmentalist and Nobel Peace Prize winner known for her work in environmental conservation, women's rights, and sustainable development through the Green Belt Movement.

Wangari Maathai, born on April 1, 1940, in Ihithe, Kenya, was a pioneering environmental and political activist. Growing up in a rural farming community, she developed a deep connection with nature. Her academic journey took her to the United States in 1960, where she earned a bachelor's degree in biological sciences from Mount St. Scholastica College and a Master of Science from the University of Pittsburgh. Returning to Kenya, she became the first woman in East and Central Africa to earn a Ph.D., receiving her doctorate in veterinary anatomy from the University of Nairobi in 1971.

Maathai's scientific background and deep understanding of ecological systems led her to found the Green Belt Movement in 1977. This environmental organization focused on tree planting, environmental conservation, and women's rights. It aimed to combat deforestation and soil erosion while empowering rural women through training and economic opportunities.

Her environmental activism soon crossed with political activism, as she criticized the Kenyan government's environmental policies and corruption. She led several high-profile campaigns, including successful efforts to halt the construction of a skyscraper in Nairobi's Uhuru Park and to stop deforestation in Karura Forest. Despite facing harassment, imprisonment, and physical violence, Maathai remained dedicated to her cause.

In 2004, Maathai was awarded the Nobel Peace Prize for her contributions to sustainable development, democracy, and peace. She was the first African woman and the first environmentalist to receive this honour. Her Nobel Prize brought global attention to her work and the crucial link between environmental sustainability and peace.

Beyond her environmental work, Maathai served as an Assistant Minister for Environment and Natural Resources in Kenya and was a member of parliament for Tetu constituency. She authored several books, including her memoir, "Unbowed," and received numerous awards and honours.

Wangari Maathai passed away on September 25, 2011, but her legacy endures through the ongoing efforts of the Green Belt Movement and the inspiration she continues to provide to environmental and social activists worldwide. Her story is a testament to flexibility, courage, and the profound impact of grassroots activism in protecting our planet and advocating for human rights.

One of the most compelling stories associated with Wangari Maathai is her courageous stand against the Kenyan government's plan to construct a skyscraper in Nairobi's Uhuru Park. This episode highlights her fearless activism and commitment to environmental conservation.

In the late 1980s, the Kenyan government, under President Daniel arap Moi, proposed the construction of a massive, 60-story office complex in Uhuru Park, a significant green space in Nairobi. The project, known as the Times Tower, was backed by powerful political and business interests and was set to encroach upon one of the city's few remaining public parks.

Wangari Maathai, recognizing the environmental and social implications of this project, launched a campaign to oppose it. She argued that the construction would not only destroy a vital green space but also set a dangerous precedent for the exploitation of public land. Despite facing intense pressure and opposition, Maathai remained resolute in her stand.

Her activism brought her into direct conflict with the government. She faced harassment, threats, and even physical violence. At one point, she was publicly denounced by the government, which attempted to discredit her and her work. Maathai, however, was undeterred. She mobilized public opinion, rallied support from international environmental organizations, and used the media to highlight the issue.

In a dramatic turn of events, Maathai wrote an open letter to the then-president of Kenya, urging him to reconsider the project. She also organized protests and marches, despite the personal risk involved. Her efforts paid off when, in 1989, the government announced the cancellation of the skyscraper project, citing financial reasons and public opposition.

This victory was a significant moment in Kenya's environmental history and showcased Maathai's unwavering dedication to environmental conservation and her ability to mobilize grassroots support. It also highlighted the importance of preserving public spaces for future generations.

The Uhuru Park campaign was one of many battles Maathai fought in her lifelong commitment to environmental and social justice. Her success in this endeavour not only saved a crucial green space but also inspired countless others to stand up for the environment and human rights.

9. PROMINENT THINKERS ADORNED AS MORTAL GODS

Prominent thinkers who have significantly influenced humanity and are often revered for their contributions to philosophy, science, ethics, and social justice are sometimes metaphorically referred to as "mortal gods." These individuals have left a profound legacy through their ground-breaking ideas and actions. Here are a few examples:

SOCRATES

Socrates was an ancient Greek philosopher who is considered one of the founders of Western philosophy. Known for his method of inquiry and dialogue, he focused on ethics and the examination of moral virtues. His teachings influenced his student Plato and, subsequently, the entire Western philosophical tradition.

Socrates, one of the most influential philosophers in Western history, lived in ancient Athens during the 5th century BC. Born around 470/469 BC in Alopece to a stonecutter named Sophroniscus and a midwife named Phaenarete, not much is known about his early life, but it is believed that he received a basic education typical of Athenian boys at the time. He married Xanthippe, who is often depicted as a troublesome wife in later accounts, and they had three sons: Lamprocles, Sophroniscus, and Menexenus. Socrates served as a hoplite (a heavily armed foot soldier) in the Athenian military and participated in several campaigns during the Peloponnesian War, including the battles at Potidaea, Delium, and Amphipolis. He was known for his bravery and stamina, qualities that his fellow soldier Alcibiades praised in Plato's dialogues.

Socrates did not write down his teachings, and what we know of him comes from the accounts of his students, particularly Plato and Xenophon, as well as the playwright Aristophanes. He is best known for his method of inquiry, the Socratic Method, which involved asking a series of questions to stimulate critical thinking and illuminate ideas. He used this method to explore ethical concepts such as justice, virtue, and devotion. He spent much of his time in public spaces like the marketplace, engaging Athenians in philosophical discussions, believing in the pursuit of knowledge and self-examination, famously stating, "The unexamined life is not worth living." His approach often exposed the ignorance of his interlocutors, which made him both respected and resented.

Socrates had a significant impact on many young Athenians, and his most famous students included Plato and Xenophon. Plato would go on to write numerous dialogues featuring Socrates as the main character, thus preserving his teacher's ideas and methods for posterity. Another student, Aristippus, founded the Cyrenaic school of philosophy, and Antisthenes laid the groundwork for Cynicism. In 399 BC, Socrates was brought to trial on charges of corrupting the youth of Athens and wickedness, specifically not recognizing the gods of the state and introducing new deities. His accusers, Meletus, Anytus, and Lycon, likely had political motivations, as Socrates was associated with several individuals who had been involved in the oligarchic regime of the Thirty Tyrants, which had briefly ruled Athens.

During the trial, as recounted in Plato's "Apology," Socrates defended himself with characteristic wit and logic, questioning the validity of the charges and the motives of his accusers. He argued that he was fulfilling a divine mission to encourage Athenians to seek virtue and wisdom. Despite his compelling defence, the jury found him guilty. When asked to propose a penalty, Socrates suggested that he be rewarded for his service to the state with free meals for life. This suggestion was seen as arrogant, and he was ultimately sentenced to death by drinking a mixture containing poison hemlock. In Plato's "Phaedo," Socrates is depicted as calmly accepting his fate, engaging in philosophical discussions with his followers until his final moments. He died surrounded by friends, maintaining his commitment to his principles to the end.

Socrates' legacy is immense, shaping the course of Western philosophy. His focus on ethics, his method of inquiry, and his commitment to questioning assumptions laid the groundwork for subsequent philosophical thought. Plato's dialogues ensured that Socratic ideas would continue to be studied and debated for millennia. Socrates' life and death highlight the tension between individual conscience and state authority, the pursuit of truth, and the nature of virtue. His influence can be seen in various philosophical traditions, from the Cynics and Stoics to modern existentialism and analytic philosophy, making him a symbol of intellectual integrity and the enduring quest for knowledge.

there are several stories and anecdotes associated with Socrates that illustrate his personality, philosophy, and interactions with others:

The Delphic Oracle

One of the most famous stories about Socrates involves the Oracle of Delphi. According to Plato's "Apology," Chaerephon, a friend of Socrates, asked the Oracle if there was anyone wiser than Socrates. The Oracle replied that there was no one wiser. Perplexed by this answer, Socrates embarked on a mission to find someone wiser than himself. This quest led him to question many Athenians, including politicians, poets, and craftsmen, ultimately leading him to conclude that while he was not wise, he was at least aware of his own ignorance.

Socratic Irony

Socrates often used a technique called irony, where he pretended to be ignorant or to ask naive questions to provoke deeper thinking in his interlocutors. This method can be seen in many of Plato's dialogues, where Socrates engages in discussions with various Athenians, exposing contradictions in their beliefs and assumptions.

The Trial and Defence

The trial and defence of Socrates, as depicted in Plato's "Apology," is itself a dramatic story. Socrates is accused of corrupting the youth of Athens and introducing new gods. During the trial, Socrates defends himself with logic and wit, challenging the validity of the charges and the motives of his accusers. Despite his efforts, the jury finds him guilty, and he is sentenced to death.

The Death of Socrates

The death of Socrates, as recounted in Plato's "Phaedo," is a poignant and philosophical moment. Socrates accepts his fate calmly, engaging in philosophical discussions with his followers until his final moments. He drinks the hemlock poison as a final act of obedience to the laws of Athens, maintaining his commitment to his principles even in death.

Socratic Legacy

After his death, Socrates' legacy continued through his students, particularly Plato and Xenophon, who wrote about his teachings and preserved his ideas for future generations. Plato's dialogues, in particular, present Socrates as a central character, embodying his method of inquiry and exploring his philosophy.

These stories and anecdotes not only illustrate Socrates' life and philosophy but also highlight his enduring influence on Western thought and intellectual history. Socrates' commitment to questioning assumptions, seeking wisdom, and facing death with integrity has inspired countless thinkers and philosophers throughout history.

PLATO

A student of Socrates and a teacher of Aristotle, Plato founded the Academy in Athens, one of the earliest institutions of higher learning. His works, including "The Republic," explored justice, the ideal state, and the nature of reality and knowledge.

Plato, one of the most influential philosophers in Western history, was born around 428/427 BC in Athens,

Greece, to an aristocratic family with connections to both Solon and the early kings of Athens. His birth name was Aristocles, but he later acquired the nickname "Plato," possibly meaning "broad" or "wide," which may have referred to his robust physique or broad forehead.

Plato belonged to a distinguished Athenian family and received a classical education typical of young Athenian aristocrats, which included grammar, music, gymnastics, and mathematics. He was also trained in wrestling and had a strong interest in both poetry and philosophy.

Plato's introduction to philosophy came through his encounter with Socrates, whom he met when he was about 20 years old. Socrates became Plato's mentor and deeply influenced his thinking and approach to philosophy. Plato was captivated by Socrates' method of questioning and dialogue, which sought to elicit wisdom and knowledge from others by asking probing questions and challenging assumptions.

After Socrates' death in 399 BC, Plato travelled extensively, including visits to Egypt, Italy, and Sicily. During these travels, he encountered various schools of thought, including Pythagoreanism and Eleaticism, which further shaped his philosophical views.

Upon returning to Athens, Plato founded the Academy around 387 BC, which is often considered the first institution of higher learning in the Western world. The Academy provided a place for intellectuals to engage in philosophical discussion and research, and it remained operational for nearly 900 years.

Plato's philosophical writings are in the form of dialogues, where characters discuss philosophical issues and concepts. These dialogues often feature Socrates as the main character, portraying his conversations with various interlocutors on topics ranging from justice and virtue to knowledge and the nature of reality.

One of Plato's most famous and influential works is "The Republic," where he outlines his vision of an ideal society governed by philosopher-kings. In this work, Plato explores the nature of justice, the role of the individual in the state, and the relationship between knowledge and governance.

Another important dialogue is "Phaedo," which recounts the final hours of Socrates' life, including his discussions on the immortality of the soul and the afterlife. This dialogue reflects Plato's own views on metaphysics and the nature of reality.

Plato's philosophy is characterized by his theory of Forms, or Ideas, which suggests that the material world is an imperfect reflection of an ideal empire of timeless, unchanging Forms. According to Plato, true knowledge comes from grasping these Forms through rational thought and dialectical reasoning.

In addition to his philosophical works, Plato wrote extensively on topics such as ethics, politics, aesthetics, epistemology, and metaphysics. His writings continue to be studied and debated by philosophers, scholars, and students around the world.

Plato died around 348/347 BC in Athens, leaving behind a rich legacy of philosophical thought and inquiry. His influence on Western philosophy, education, and intellectual discourse cannot be overstated, as his ideas have shaped the development of philosophy and influenced countless thinkers throughout history.

One notable incident from Plato's life involves his travels to Sicily, where he visited the court of Dionysius I of Syracuse. Plato, with his idealistic belief that philosophy could guide rulers to govern wisely, sought to influence Dionysius and instil in him philosophical wisdom. However, Plato's attempts were met with scepticism and resistance from the dictatorial ruler.

Dionysius, not appreciating Plato's philosophical ideas and perhaps threatened by his influence, reportedly sold Plato into slavery. Plato was eventually rescued and returned to Athens through the efforts of his friends and supporters. This experience left a lasting impression on Plato, shaping his views on the difficulties of applying philosophical principles in political contexts and the challenges of educating rulers to embrace wisdom and justice.

Plato's trip to Sicily underscores the complexities and dangers faced by philosophers who sought to engage with political leaders and influence governance through philosophical ideals. Despite this setback, Plato continued to develop his philosophical teachings and writings, which would profoundly influence Western philosophy for centuries to come. His dialogues, including "The Republic," "Phaedo," and "Symposium," remain foundational texts in the history of philosophy, exploring profound questions about justice, virtue, the nature of reality, and the pursuit of wisdom.

ARISTOTLE

A student of Plato and tutor to Alexander the Great, Aristotle made significant contributions to numerous fields, including metaphysics, ethics, politics, and natural sciences. His works laid the foundation for much of Western thought and scientific inquiry.

Aristotle, one of the most influential philosophers, scientists, and educators in Western history, was born in 384 BC in Stagira, a Greek city on the northern Aegean coast. His father, Nicomachus, was a court physician to the Macedonian king Amyntas II, which provided Aristotle with early exposure to medicine and biology.

At the age of 17, Aristotle moved to Athens to study at Plato's Academy, where he remained for nearly 20 years until Plato's death in 347 BC. Aristotle's time at the Academy had a profound impact on his philosophical development, although he did not always agree with Plato's teachings, particularly on the theory of Forms. After Plato's death, Aristotle left Athens and spent several years traveling and studying, possibly in Asia Minor and the islands of the Aegean Sea.

Around 343 BC, Aristotle was invited by King Philip II of Macedon to tutor his son, the future Alexander the Great, who was then a young boy. Aristotle returned to Macedonia and became Alexander's tutor for several years, educating him in a wide range of subjects, including philosophy, rhetoric, and the natural sciences. This period was formative for both Aristotle and Alexander, as Aristotle's teachings laid the foundation for Alexander's future conquests and the spread of Greek culture throughout the known world.

In 335 BC, Aristotle returned to Athens and founded his own school, the Lyceum, which became one of the most prominent philosophical and scientific institutions of antiquity. Unlike Plato's Academy, which focused more on abstract philosophical inquiries, the Lyceum emphasized empirical observation, classification, and the study of natural phenomena. Aristotle and his students conducted research in biology, zoology, botany, physics, astronomy, and other disciplines, laying the groundwork for many scientific principles that would later become central to Western thought.

Aristotle's philosophical works cover a wide range of subjects, including metaphysics, ethics, politics, rhetoric, poetics, and logic. His essays on ethics, such as the "Nicomachean Ethics" and "Eudemian Ethics," explore the nature of virtue, happiness, and the good life. In his work "Politics," Aristotle examines different forms of government and proposes his famous idea of the "best regime," which he argues is a mixture of monarchy, aristocracy, and democracy.

Aristotle's contributions to logic are foundational to the development of Western philosophy and science. His work "Organon" lays out the basic principles of deductive reasoning and the syllogism, which became the standard tools of logical analysis for over two millennia. In metaphysics, Aristotle explores the nature of being, substance, causality, and the relationship between form and matter.

After Alexander's death in 323 BC, anti-Macedonian sentiment forced Aristotle to leave Athens, and he died in Euboea the following year. His works were preserved and studied throughout the Middle Ages by Islamic and Christian scholars, who saw him as the pinnacle of human knowledge and understanding. In the Renaissance, Aristotle's works were rediscovered and became a central part of European intellectual life, influencing figures such as Thomas Aquinas, Dante Alighieri, and Francis Bacon.

Aristotle's legacy continues to be felt today in philosophy, science, and education. His emphasis on empirical observation, logical reasoning, and systematic classification laid the groundwork for modern scientific inquiry, while his ethical and political theories continue to provoke debate and discussion. Aristotle remains one of the towering figures in the history of Western thought, whose influence on subsequent generations cannot be overstated.

One of the notable stories from Aristotle's life is his involvement in the Contest of Delos, which is recounted by several ancient sources, including Diogenes Laërtius and Plutarch.

In 343 BC, Aristotle and his fellow philosophers at the Academy in Athens were invited to participate in the Contest of Delos, a prestigious religious and cultural festival held in honour of the god Apollo. The festival featured competitions in music, drama, and philosophy, with contestants traveling from all over Greece to showcase their talents.

At the time, Aristotle was a student at Plato's Academy, and he competed against several other philosophers in the philosophical contest. Each contestant was given a theme to develop and present in front of a panel of judges and a large audience. Aristotle's rhetorical and philosophical skills were put to the test as he debated and argued his points against other prominent philosophers of the day.

According to tradition, Aristotle delivered a powerful and persuasive speech that impressed the judges and won him the first prize. His victory in the Contest of Delos not only brought him acclaim and recognition but also demonstrated his prowess in rhetoric and philosophy at a young age.

This event is significant not only for Aristotle's personal achievements but also for showcasing the intellectual vitality of Athens during the classical period. It highlights Aristotle's early talent and ambition, as well as his ability to engage in philosophical debate and discourse, which would become central to his later career as a philosopher, scientist, and educator.

The Contest of Delos marked an important milestone in Aristotle's life, setting the stage for his future contributions to philosophy and science. It also reflects the competitive and intellectually stimulating environment of ancient Greek society, where philosophical debate and inquiry were highly valued and celebrated.

10. PHILOSOPHER AND THINKERS

CONFUCIUS

Confucius was a Chinese philosopher whose teachings emphasized personal and governmental morality, correctness of social relationships, justice, and sincerity. His philosophy, known as Confucianism, has deeply influenced Chinese culture and other East Asian countries.

Certainly! Confucius, whose birth name was Kong Qiu and who is also known as Kong Fuzi or Master Kong, lived during the Spring and Autumn Period of Chinese history, between 551 and 479 BC. He was born in the state of Lu, located in present-day Shandong Province, China. Despite being born into a noble family that had fallen on hard times, Confucius received a solid education in the traditional arts and humanities of ancient China. This upbringing instilled in him a deep reverence for learning and a strong sense of moral duty from a young age.

As a young man, Confucius began his career in public service, holding various government positions in Lu. However, he grew increasingly disillusioned with the political turmoil and moral decline he witnessed. Confucius believed that the solution to the problems of his time lay in the restoration of ethical principles and the cultivation of virtuous leadership.

Central to Confucius's teachings is the concept of Ren, often translated as "benevolence" or "humaneness." Ren emphasizes the importance of treating others with kindness, sympathy, and respect. It serves as the cornerstone of Confucian ethics, guiding individuals towards moral excellence and harmonious relationships within society.

Another key concept in Confucian thought is Li, which refers to ritual propriety, etiquette, and proper conduct in various social contexts. Li emphasizes the significance of observing traditions and rituals as a means of cultivating moral character and maintaining social order.

Confucius also stressed the virtue of Xiao, or family devotion, which underscores the respect and care one should have for parents and ancestors. Xiao is seen as fundamental to building strong family relationships and fostering social harmony.

Throughout his life, Confucius travelled extensively, imparting his teachings to eager disciples and seeking to influence rulers and officials. Despite facing rejection and misunderstanding during his lifetime, his ideas gradually gained grip and became foundational to Chinese philosophy and culture.

Confucius's legacy extends beyond his own era. After his death in 479 BC, his disciples compiled his teachings into the Analects, a collection of sayings and dialogues that preserved his philosophy for future generations. Confucianism became the dominant philosophical and ethical system in China, influencing not only moral thought and personal conduct but also governance, education, and social relationships.

Today, Confucianism continues to exert a profound influence in East Asia and beyond. It exemplifies principles of ethics, morality, and social harmony, offering insights into the cultivation of personal virtue and the promotion of a just and harmonious society.

During his time as a government official in the state of Lu, Confucius served in various roles, aiming to implement his ideas of ethical governance and moral leadership. However, his efforts were met with resistance and opposition from those who were rooted in the existing power structures and political competitions.

At one point, Confucius held a prominent position as Minister of Crime in Lu. He sought to reform the justice system by emphasizing moral education and ethical conduct among officials. Confucius believed that if officials were virtuous and acted with integrity, they could govern justly and inspire others to do the same.

Despite his sincere efforts, Confucius faced strong opposition and hostility from corrupt officials and those who preferred the status quo. His proposals for reform were often ignored or rejected, and he encountered personal attacks and threats to his safety.

Despite these challenges, Confucius remained steadfast in his convictions and continued to advocate for his principles. He refused to compromise his values or abandon his belief in the transformative power of education and ethical leadership. There is very interesting story of his childhood called "The tale of the lost lamb".

The Tale of the Lost Lamb

When Confucius was a young boy, he lived in a small village surrounded by hills and farmlands. One day, the village elders announced that a lamb belonging to a poor farmer had wandered off and was lost. The lamb was vital to the farmer's livelihood, so everyone was asked to help search for it.

Confucius eagerly joined the search party, though some older children scoffed, saying, "What can a little boy like you do?" But Confucius replied, **"Even small efforts can bring big results when done with sincerity."**

He spent hours looking, paying attention to places no one else thought to check. At last, in a quiet thicket near the edge of the forest, he spotted the lamb, tangled in some bushes. Gently freeing it, he carried it back to the farmer.

The villagers were overjoyed, and the farmer wept with gratitude. But when people praised him, young Confucius said, **"I only did what I hope others would do for me if I needed help. Everyone's effort matters."**

ISAAC NEWTON

An English mathematician, physicist, and astronomer who is widely recognized for his work on the laws of motion and universal gravitation. His book "Mathematical Principles of Natural Philosophy" laid the groundwork for classical mechanics.

Isaac Newton, born on January 4, 1643, in Woolsthorpe, Lincolnshire, England, became a major figure in science, famous for his big contributions to physics, mathematics, and astronomy. He faced challenges early in life; he was orphaned as a child but showed a natural curiosity and talent for learning. He started his education at the King's School in Grantham, where his skill in mathematics stood out, leading him to join Trinity College, Cambridge.

At Cambridge, Newton explored the scientific ideas of his time, studying the works of great thinkers like Galileo, Descartes, and Kepler. During the plague years of 1665–1666, Newton went back home, a time known as his "year of wonders." During this period, he made key discoveries in mathematics, creating his calculus theories, which are the basis of modern calculus today.

Newton didn't just focus on mathematics. His experiments with light and color led to his important book, Opticks, published in 1704. In this book, he showed how light is made up of different colors using prisms and lenses. He also invented the reflecting telescope, which highlighted his expertise in optics and confirmed his status as a top scientist of his time.

However, Newton's most lasting legacy is his monumental book, Philosophiæ Naturalis Principia Mathematica (Mathematical Principles of Natural Philosophy), published in 1687. In this magnum opus, Newton formulated his laws of motion and universal gravitation, which provided a comprehensive framework for understanding the motion of celestial bodies and earthly objects alike. His laws of motion elucidated the fundamental relationships between force, mass, and acceleration, establishing the principles of classical mechanics that dominated scientific thought for centuries.

Newton's influence extended beyond theoretical physics; his appointment as the Lucasian Professor of Mathematics at Cambridge in 1669 marked the beginning of a distinguished academic career. Later in life, Newton served as Master of the Royal Mint, where he played a crucial role in reforming Britain's currency and combating fake practices.

Isaac Newton passed away on March 31, 1727, leaving behind a legacy that remains indelibly etched in the records of scientific history. His rigorous methodology, emphasis on experiential evidence, and profound insights into the workings of the natural world laid the groundwork for the scientific revolution and shaped the course of scientific inquiry for generations to come. Newton's contributions continue to inspire scientists, scholars, and thinkers worldwide, underscoring his status as a visionary whose intellectual prowess transformed our understanding of the universe.

One of the most famous stories associated with Isaac Newton is the legend of the falling apple, which is often cited as an inspiration for his theory of gravitation. According to the popular account, Newton was sitting under an apple tree in his garden at Woolsthorpe Manor, contemplating the forces of nature. As he looked up, he observed an apple fall from the tree to the ground. This simple observation sparked a moment of insight for Newton: he began to ponder whether the same force that caused the apple to fall also governed the motion of the Moon and planets.

This moment of contemplation led Newton to formulate his theory of universal gravitation. He realized that the force pulling the apple towards the Earth's surface (gravity) was not limited to apples or Earth alone, but extended throughout the universe. Newton's ground-breaking insight was that every object with mass attracts every other object with a force that is proportional to the product of their masses and in reverse proportional to the square of the distance between their centres.

Although the story of the falling apple has become a legendary anecdote, historians debate its factual accuracy. It is more likely that Newton's understanding of gravity evolved through rigorous experimentation, mathematical reasoning, and observations rather than a single moment of inspiration. Nevertheless, the story of the apple serves as a powerful symbol of Newton's genius and his ability to derive profound scientific insights from everyday observations.

This legend underscores Newton's methodical approach to scientific inquiry and his ability to synthesize complex phenomena into elegant mathematical formulations. It continues to capture the imagination of people around the world, illustrating how pivotal moments of observation and reflection can lead to transformative discoveries in science and beyond.

Isaac Newton, celebrated for his profound contributions to science and mathematics, faced notable opposition and challenges throughout his illustrious career. Despite his ground-breaking achievements, Newton encountered criticism, particularly when he published his important work, Philosophiæ Naturalis Principia Mathematica, in 1687. This monumental essay presented Newton's laws of motion and universal gravitation, revolutionizing our understanding of physics and celestial mechanics. However, Newton's theories challenged existing frameworks, especially those advocated by Cartesian philosophers, leading to debates and resistance within the scientific community.

While at the University of Cambridge, where Newton held the important role of Lucasian Professor of Mathematics, he had many academic arguments and conflicts. The most notable was his prolonged feud with Gottfried Wilhelm Leibniz over the invention of calculus, which involved both mathematicians in accusations of plagiarism and priority disputes.

Aside from intellectual challenges, Newton also faced political difficulties when he was the Master of the

Royal Mint. He was in charge of reforming Britain's coins and fighting against counterfeiting, but he met resistance from established interests and government obstacles, showing the broader political stresses of his period.

On a personal level, Newton's intense dedication to his work and his somewhat isolated nature sometimes strained his relationships. His intense focus on science often overshadowed social interactions, causing difficulties in his relationships with colleagues, friends, and family members.

Despite these challenges, Newton's precise thinking, ground-breaking discoveries, and relentless pursuit of knowledge ultimately prevailed. His laws of motion, theory of gravity, and optical contributions laid the foundation for modern physics and influenced many generations of scientists. Newton's legacy remains as proof of the power of intellect, perseverance, and the transformative impact of scientific inquiry on understanding the natural world.

IMMANUEL KANT

A German philosopher who is a central figure in modern philosophy. His works, including the "Critique of Pure Reason," have influenced various fields such as metaphysics, epistemology, ethics, and political theory.

Immanuel Kant was born on April 22, 1724, in Königsberg, Prussia, now Kaliningrad, Russia. He was the fourth of nine children in a modest family, and his parents were sincere followers of the Pietist branch of Protestantism. His father was a harness maker, and his mother was known for her religious devotion and strong moral character, traits that greatly influenced Kant throughout his life.

Kant's early education was rigorous and deeply religious, focusing on Latin, the Bible, and classical literature. In 1740, at the age of sixteen, he enrolled at the University of Königsberg, initially studying theology but quickly towards mathematics and physics, inspired by the work of Isaac Newton.

After university, Kant spent several years working as a private tutor before returning to academia. He earned his doctorate in 1755 and began lecturing at the University of Königsberg. During this period, Kant wrote extensively on a wide range of subjects, including physics, astronomy, and philosophy, but it was his work in the latter that would earn him lasting fame.

Kant's critical period began in the 1780s when he published "Critique of Pure Reason" in 1781. This seminal work sought to resolve the conflict between rationalist and experimenter traditions by arguing that while all our knowledge begins with experience, not all of it arises from experience. He introduced the concept of inspiring idealism, proposing that our experience of things is about how they appear to us, shaped by our perceptions, rather than about those things as they are in themselves.

Kant continued to develop his philosophical ideas in subsequent works, including the "Critique of Practical Reason" (1788), which focused on ethics, and the "Critique of Judgment" (1790), which dealt with aesthetics and teleology. His moral philosophy, particularly the concept of the categorical imperative, has been profoundly influential.

This principle asserts that one should act only according to sayings that could be universal laws, emphasizing duty and the basic worth of human beings.

Throughout his life, Kant was known for his disciplined and predictable lifestyle. He never married and rarely left his hometown, spending his days writing, lecturing, and engaging in philosophical discussions. Despite his relatively uneventful personal life, his intellectual contributions were revolutionary, shaping modern philosophy and influencing countless thinkers.

Kant passed away on February 12, 1804, in Königsberg. His ideas continue to resonate, underscoring his belief in the power of reason and the potential for human progress. His work laid the foundation for various fields within philosophy and inspired later movements, including German Idealism and existentialism.

One notable incident in Immanuel Kant's life was the disruption of his famously regimented daily routine due to the impact of reading a book. Kant was known for his incredibly disciplined lifestyle, which included a strict schedule that he rarely deviated from. He would rise at 5 AM, lecture at the university, work on his writings, and take his daily walks at the same time every day, becoming so predictable that the townspeople of Königsberg reportedly set their clocks by his walks.

However, in 1762, this routine was disrupted when Kant read Jean-Jacques Rousseau's "Emile, or On

Education." The ideas presented in Rousseau's work profoundly affected Kant, causing him to reconsider many of his own thoughts on human nature and society. Rousseau's emphasis on the importance of education and the natural goodness of humans inspired Kant to delve deeper into questions about human freedom and morality.

This intellectual engagement with Rousseau's ideas was so consuming that Kant reportedly skipped his daily walk for several days, an extraordinary break from his usual habits. This incident highlights the profound impact that Rousseau's philosophy had on Kant, shaping his own philosophical inquiries and contributing to the development of his later works.

This episode illustrates not only the power of intellectual influence but also the depth of Kant's commitment to exploring and understanding complex ideas, even at the expense of his famously strict routine. This story shows that even the most disciplined people can lose themselves in passion. Kant teaches us two powerful lessons:

1. **Consistency is Strength**: Success isn't about being perfect but about showing up daily for what you believe in—whether it's studying, creating, or pursuing a dream.

2. **Curiosity Fuels Passion:** Even a routine-driven philosopher like Kant could get so excited about learning that he forgot his routine. It's a reminder that curiosity and learning make life exciting.

So, next time you're working on a project or trying to develop a new habit, think of Kant, the man who balanced discipline with a passion for ideas. Maybe you, too, can inspire others with your dedication!

SWAMI VIVEKANAD

Swami Vivekananda, born as Narendra Nath Dutta in Kolkata, was a boy full of curiosity and energy. From a young age, he was fascinated by big questions about life, God, and the universe. He loved reading books and learning about different subjects, but one question always troubled him: "Have you seen God?"

As he grew older, Narendra heard about a saint named Ramakrishna Paramahamsa, who lived in a nearby temple. Eager to find answers, he went to meet him and asked directly, "Have you seen God?" To his amazement, Ramakrishna replied calmly, "Yes, I have seen God. I see Him as clearly as I see you." This answer deeply impacted Narendra, and he started visiting Ramakrishna regularly. Over time, he became Ramakrishna's disciple and learned that God resides in everyone and that serving people selflessly is the highest form of devotion.

After Ramakrishna passed away, Narendra took the path of a monk and adopted the name Swami Vivekananda. He travelled across India to understand the lives of ordinary people. What he saw broke his heart—poverty, hunger, and suffering were everywhere. He realized that India needed education, unity, and self-confidence to rise again. He often encouraged people with his famous words: "Arise, awake, and stop not till the goal is reached!"

In 1893, Swami Vivekananda attended the Parliament of Religions in Chicago to share India's spiritual wisdom with the world. When he stood to speak, he began with the words, "Sisters and Brothers of America," which immediately won the hearts of the audience. He spoke about harmony among religions, peace, and the idea that all faiths lead to the same truth. His speech made him an international figure, and people from across the globe sought to learn from him.

This greeting was special because, at that time, people from different countries usually addressed audiences in formal or distant terms, like **"Ladies and Gentlemen"** or **"Honorable guests."** But Swami Vivekananda used the word "Sisters and Brothers," making everyone feel like part of a big family, no matter where they came from. He spoke to them with love and respect, showing that, despite cultural differences, all human beings are connected and equal.

The audience was deeply moved by this warmth and friendliness. It made them feel that he was speaking not just to a group of strangers, but to them as equals, as members of a global human family. They clapped and cheered, not just for his greeting, but for the way he made them feel connected and valued in that moment. This simple yet powerful way of addressing people opened their hearts and made his speech even more memorable.

In his speech, Swami Vivekananda spoke about the universal values shared by all religions, such as love, compassion, and respect for humanity. He emphasized that **"all religions are true"** and that no one religion should claim to be the only path to God. His message was one of tolerance, peace, and harmony between different faiths. He stressed that **religion is not just about rituals** or outward practices, but about experiencing the divine truth within oneself.

Vivekananda also talked about the ancient wisdom of India, particularly the teachings of Vedanta and Yoga, which he presented to understand and experience the universal truth beyond cultural differences. He urged the audience to recognize the unity of all religions and to focus on serving humanity.

The speech was revolutionary at the time, as it promoted a message of unity in diversity, respect for all religions, and the importance of spiritual development. The audience responded with a standing ovation, deeply moved by his powerful words and vision for a more inclusive and peaceful world.

During one of his travels in India, Narendranath was on a train, dressed in simple traditional Indian attire. In the same compartment were a group of English-speaking passengers. Seeing his modest appearance, they assumed he was an uneducated villager and began mocking him in English.

They spoke loudly, making rude remarks about Indians, and laughed at his expense, believing he couldn't understand a word they were saying.

Narendranath sat quietly, listening to everything without reacting. But after some time, he turned to them and, in flawless English, said with a calm smile, **"Gentlemen, it seems you are quite entertained by your assumptions about me. Perhaps I should now speak in your language so you can truly understand me."**

The passengers were stunned. Not only did Narendranath speak perfect English, but his confidence and dignified manner left them embarrassed. Realizing their mistake, they quickly apologized and began treating him with respect.

Upon returning to India, he inspired people to work for the upliftment of society. He founded the Ramakrishna Mission, an organization dedicated to helping the poor, educating the youth, and spreading spiritual knowledge. Swami Vivekananda believed that true service to God is found in serving humanity.

Although he passed away at the young age of 39, Swami Vivekananda left a legacy that continues to inspire millions. His life was a beacon of hope, teaching us that with faith, hard work, and compassion, we can achieve greatness and create a better world.

DR.B.R.AMBEDKAR

Father of the Indian Constitution

Dr. B.R. Ambedkar's childhood was filled with hardship and suffering, but it also showed his strength and determination to rise above adversity.

Bhimrao Ambedkar was born on April 14, 1891, in a small village called Mhow in present-day Madhya Pradesh, India. His family was part of the Mahar caste, which at that time was considered "untouchable" by society. People from this caste were treated very badly, and even though Bhim's family was poor, they had to endure even more disrespect because of their caste.

As a young child, Bhim faced many challenges. At school, other children wouldn't let him sit with them or drink water from the same well. The teachers also treated him unfairly. Bhim was often called names and made to feel like he was less than the others. But despite all this cruelty, Bhim never gave up on his dream of getting an education.

Bhim's father, who had served in the British army, was one of the few people in his family who could read and write. He encouraged Bhim to study and gave him books. Bhim loved to read and would often study late into the night. His family, despite their struggles, supported his education.

Bhim's early education was not easy. He was the only Dalit student in his class, which meant he was often excluded and treated badly. But he was determined to do well. In 1907, he went to a school in Bombay (now Mumbai), where he faced even more discrimination. He was not allowed to sit with the other students in the class or use the same facilities, but he kept his focus on learning.

Bhim's hard work paid off when he went abroad to study. In 1912, he went to Columbia University in the United

States, where he earned his master's degree. Later, he went to London to study law at the famous London School of Economics. It was here that he became more and more passionate about fighting for the rights of the oppressed and downtrodden people.

Despite the challenges he faced growing up, Bhimrao Ambedkar never stopped fighting for his education. His determination helped him become one of the most educated and powerful leaders in Indian history. His childhood suffering shaped his mission to bring equality to the oppressed and to fight against injustice throughout his life.

Why Ambedkar Earned the Title "Father of the Indian Constitution"?

Dr. B.R. Ambedkar is celebrated as the Father of the Indian Constitution for his pivotal role in shaping the nation's governing document. His journey to this monumental achievement was characterized by his exceptional expertise and unwavering commitment to social justice.

Ambedkar's primary goal was to enshrine equality and social justice within the Constitution. He was adamant that the document should guarantee equal rights and protections for everyone, particularly those who had endured centuries of oppression, such as the Dalits, formerly known as "Untouchables." Ambedkar included provisions to abolish untouchability and caste-based discrimination, striving to create a society where all individuals could live with dignity and equal rights.

One of Ambedkar's significant contributions was the inclusion of Fundamental Rights in the Constitution. These rights, including equality, freedom of speech, and protection from discrimination, became the bedrock of India's democratic system. Ambedkar meticulously ensured these rights were clearly articulated, empowering every Indian citizen to seek justice if their rights were violated.

Furthermore, Ambedkar championed social reforms to uplift marginalized communities. He advocated for affirmative action in education and employment, leading to the establishment of reservation (quota) systems for underrepresented groups. This policy continues to play a crucial role in India's public institutions, promoting social inclusion and equality.

Ambedkar's work in drafting the Constitution laid the foundation for a democratic India governed by the rule of law. His vision for a just and equal society, combined with his intellectual prowess, solidified his legacy as a principal architect of the world's largest democracy. Dr. B.R. Ambedkar's extraordinary contributions have left an enduring impact, and the Constitution remains a testament to his dedication to justice, equality, and social reform.

Dr. B.R. Ambedkar is called the Father of the Indian Constitution because of his central role in drafting and shaping the Constitution of India. His leadership and contributions to the Constituent Assembly, the body responsible for creating the Constitution after India gained independence in 1947, were crucial in ensuring that the Constitution provided for justice, equality, and the protection of rights for all citizens.

Here's why Ambedkar earned this title:

1. **Chairman of the Drafting Committee**

In 1947, as India embarked on the path to becoming an independent republic, the Constituent Assembly was formed to draft the Constitution. Recognizing his profound knowledge of law, economics, and social issues, Ambedkar was appointed Chairman of the Drafting Committee. He led this group with dedication, ensuring the Constitution was fair, inclusive, and protected the rights of all citizens.

2. **Commitment to Equality and Social Justice**

Ambedkar's primary goal was to enshrine equality and social justice within the Constitution. He was adamant that the document should guarantee equal rights and protections for everyone, particularly those who had endured centuries of oppression, such as the Dalits, formerly known as "Untouchables." Ambedkar included provisions to abolish untouchability and caste-based discrimination, striving to create a society where all individuals could live with dignity and equal rights.

3. Protection of Fundamental Rights

One of Ambedkar's significant contributions was the inclusion of Fundamental Rights in the Constitution. These rights, including equality, freedom of speech, and protection from discrimination, became the bedrock of India's democratic system. Ambedkar meticulously ensured these rights were clearly articulated, empowering every Indian citizen to seek justice if their rights were violated.

4.Social Reforms

Ambedkar championed social reforms to uplift marginalized communities. He advocated for affirmative action in education and employment, leading to the establishment of reservation (quota) systems for underrepresented groups. This policy continues to play a crucial role in India's public institutions, promoting social inclusion and equality.

5.Legacy of Democracy and Rule of Law

Ambedkar's work in drafting the Constitution laid the foundation for a democratic India governed by the rule of law. His vision for a just and equal society, combined with his intellectual prowess, solidified his legacy as a principal architect of the world's largest democracy.

Because of his extraordinary intellectual contributions, his vision for a just and equal society, and his leadership in drafting the document that governs the world's largest democracy, Dr. B.R. Ambedkar is honoured as the *Father of the Indian Constitution.* His work has left a lasting legacy, and the Constitution remains a testament to his dedication to justice, equality, and social reform.

CHANAKYA

Chanakya, also known as Kautilya or Vishnugupta, was a brilliant teacher, strategist, and advisor in ancient India. His story is one of wisdom, intelligence, and perseverance. Chanakya is best known for his role in shaping the Maurya Empire, which became one of the most powerful empires in Indian history. Here's a simple story of his life:

Early Life and Challenges

Chanakya was born around 350 BCE in a small village in India. He was a brilliant student from a young age and loved learning. He went to study at the famous ancient university called **Takshashila**, where he became an expert in subjects like economics, politics, and philosophy.

But Chanakya was not just an ordinary scholar. He was very wise and had strong principles. He didn't like the way the king of his time, **Dhananandа**, was ruling his kingdom. Chanakya felt that the king was weak and unfair to his people. One day, Chanakya had enough of the king's injustice. He decided to teach him a lesson and vowed to bring a new ruler to the throne.

The Great Plan

To get rid of the bad king, Chanakya shaved his head, dressed as a humble man, and set out to find a new ruler for the kingdom. He found a young prince named **Chandragupta Maurya**, who was smart and brave. Chanakya saw the potential in him and decided to train him to become a strong and just ruler. Chanakya worked hard to teach Chandragupta everything he knew—how to manage an empire, make wise decisions, and be a fair and powerful king. With Chanakya's guidance, Chandragupta grew stronger and more confident, eventually overthrowing the weak King Dhananandа and establishing the **Maurya Empire** in 321 BCE.

Building an Empire

Chanakya became Chandragupta's trusted advisor and helped him rule the empire wisely. He made sure that the empire was well-organized, with systems for taxation, law, and order. His advice helped Chandragupta keep the empire stable and protect it from enemies.

Chanakya also wrote a famous book called the **Arthashastra**, which is a guide to managing a kingdom, handling politics, and dealing with power. The book includes advice on diplomacy, military strategy, and economics, and it is still studied today for its wisdom.

His Clever Strategies

Chanakya was known for his clever strategies and cunning tactics. One of his most famous stories is about how he defeated Alexander the Great's successors, who were trying to invade India. With his sharp mind, Chanakya managed to outsmart his enemies and protect his kingdom from foreign invaders.

He also used his intelligence to solve problems in the empire. For example, when someone tried to challenge Chandragupta's rule, Chanakya used his clever planning to neutralize the threat without violence, showing that brains could sometimes be more powerful than strength.

Legacy

Chanakya passed away around 275 BCE, but his wisdom continued to inspire generations of leaders and thinkers. His teachings about leadership, governance, and personal integrity are still relevant today. The story of Chanakya teaches us that intelligence, hard work, and determination can change the world. He showed that even if you are just one person, you can make a huge impact if you have a clear vision and the courage to act on it. His life reminds us that with the right knowledge and strategies, even the greatest challenges can be overcome.

11.SCIENTISTS AND INNOVATORS

GALILEO GALILEI

The Man Who Unveiled the Cosmos

An Italian astronomer, physicist, and engineer, often called the "father of observational astronomy," the "father of modern physics," and the "father of the scientific method." His contributions to the study of motion, astronomy, and scientific methodology were revolutionary.

Galileo Galilei, born in 1564 in Pisa, Italy, would become one of history's most influential figures in the fields of astronomy, physics, and the scientific method. His story unfolds against the backdrop of a Europe shifting from medieval traditions to the Regeneration spirit of inquiry.

From a young age, Galileo displayed a keen intellect and curiosity about the natural world. He enrolled at the University of Pisa to study medicine, as his father wished, but his interests quickly turned to mathematics and physics. This shift led him to become a professor of mathematics at the University of Padua, where he made significant advancements in the understanding of motion and procedure.

Galileo's observations with the newly invented telescope in 1609 marked a pivotal moment in his career. He turned his telescope towards the heavens and made groundbreaking discoveries. Among his observations were the craters and mountains on the Moon, the phases of Venus, and the moons of Jupiter. These observations provided evidence supporting the Copernican heliocentric model of the solar system, which posited that the Earth and planets revolve around the Sun, contrary to the geocentric model prevailing at the time.

Galileo's support for Copernican theory brought him into conflict with the Catholic Church, which held the geocentric view as doctrine. In 1616, the Church warned Galileo not to promote the heliocentric model as fact, though he continued his work. In 1632, he published his seminal work "Dialogue Concerning the Two Chief World Systems," which presented arguments for heliocentrism. This led to his trial by the Roman Investigation in 1633, where he was found "vehemently suspect of heresy" for his views and placed under house arrest for the remainder of his life.

Despite the controversies and persecution, he faced, Galileo's contributions to science continued to influence generations of thinkers. His emphasis on empirical observation, mathematical analysis, and experimental testing laid the groundwork for modern physics and astronomy. Galileo Galilei died in 1642, but his legacy as a pioneer of the scientific method and a champion of the heliocentric model endures, forever changing humanity's understanding of the universe.

One interesting story about him is how he proved that the Earth moves around the Sun. At the time, most people believed that the Earth was the center of the universe and that everything, including the Sun, revolved around it. This idea was taught by the Catholic Church, and it had been accepted for many centuries.

Galileo didn't just accept what everyone else believed. He used a telescope, which he had improved, to look at the night sky. He saw things that no one had seen before. For example, he observed that Jupiter had moons orbiting it, just like how the Earth orbits the Sun. This was important because it showed that not everything revolves around the Earth.

Galileo also looked at the Moon and saw that its surface was rough and uneven, not smooth as people once thought. He discovered sunspots on the Sun and saw that Venus went through phases, just like the Moon. All these observations helped Galileo support the idea that the Earth and other planets orbit the Sun. Unfortunately, the Church didn't like these new ideas. Galileo was told to take back what he said because it went against the teachings of the Church. But Galileo stood by his findings, and even though he was put under house arrest later in life, his work changed science forever. Today, we know that Galileo was right, and his discoveries helped lay the foundation for modern astronomy.

CHARLES DRAWIN

The Man Who Revolutionized Our Understanding of Life

An English naturalist, geologist, and biologist, best known for his contributions to the science of evolution. His book "On the Origin of Species" introduced the theory of natural selection. Charles Darwin, born on February 12,

1809, in Shrewsbury, England, was destined to become one of the most influential naturalists and scientists in history. His life's journey is marked by profound curiosity, extensive exploration, and the formulation of evolutionary theory, which revolutionized our understanding of the natural world.

Darwin grew up in a prosperous and intellectually stimulating environment. His father, Robert Darwin, was a wealthy doctor, and his grandfather, Erasmus Darwin, was a noted physician, poet, and natural philosopher. From a young age, Charles showed a keen interest in nature, often exploring the countryside around his home and collecting specimens. In 1825, Darwin enrolled at the University of Edinburgh to study medicine, following in his father's footsteps. However, he found the medical curriculum uninspiring and distasteful, leading him to pursue his true passion: natural history. In 1828, he transferred to Christ's College, Cambridge, to study theology with the intention of becoming a clergyman, a path that allowed him to indulge his interest in natural sciences.

During his time at Cambridge, Darwin was influenced by notable scientists like geologist Adam Sedgwick and botanist John Stevens Henslow, who became his mentor. In 1831, on Henslow's recommendation, Darwin joined the HMS Beagle expedition as the ship's naturalist. The five-year journey mapped the coastlines of South America and other parts of the world, profoundly shaping Darwin's scientific career. He meticulously collected specimens and made detailed observations of geology, plants, animals, and fossils. His experiences, especially in the Galápagos Islands, where he observed species variations adapted to different environments, planted the seeds for his theory of evolution by natural selection.

After returning to England in 1836, Darwin spent years analysing his findings and developing his theory of evolution. In 1859, he published "On the Origin of Species," which argued that species evolve over time through natural selection. This theory challenged creationism and provoked intense debates about life's origins. Anticipating backlash, Darwin delayed publication, aware of the potential repercussions. Critics misinterpreted his ideas, using concepts like "survival of the fittest" to justify harmful ideologies, adding complexity to public perception and further fueling controversy.

Beyond intellectual opposition, Darwin faced personal health challenges throughout his life. Chronic illnesses, particularly severe gastrointestinal issues, frequently debilitated him. Despite these setbacks, Darwin persevered in his research, driven by a deep-rooted curiosity and dedication to scientific inquiry.

Throughout his life, Darwin maintained a rigorous scientific approach, combining detailed observation with meticulous experimentation. His legacy extends beyond his theory of evolution, about contributions to fields such as botany, geology, and anthropology. Darwin died on April 19, 1882, leaving behind a legacy of scientific analysis that continues to shape our understanding of the natural world and our place within it.

Charles Darwin encountered significant challenges throughout his career, primarily restricting from the controversial nature of his theory of evolution by natural selection. His theory clashed with prevailing scientific and religious beliefs. The idea that species evolved through natural selection challenged the long-held notion of divine creation and the fixity of species. This provoked strong opposition from influential scientists and theologians who viewed evolution as contradictory to religious teachings and societal stability.

Darwin's theory of evolution revolutionized biology and had profound implications for scientific, religious, and societal perspectives. Despite controversy and criticism, Darwin continued his scientific work, publishing other influential works on subjects such as sexual selection and the expression of emotions in humans and animals.

Over time, mounting evidence from fields such as genetics, palaeontology, and comparative anatomy bolstered Darwin's theory, gradually shifting scientific consensus toward acceptance. His meticulous research and clear writing won over many sceptics. Over the years, Darwin continued to refine his ideas and published additional works, including "The Descent of Man," which applied evolutionary theory to human beings.

Charles Darwin passed away on April 19, 1882, but his legacy endures. His theory of evolution remains a cornerstone of biological sciences, influencing not only biology but also philosophy, theology, and countless other fields. Darwin's life story is a testament to the power of curiosity, perseverance, and the relentless pursuit of knowledge.

NIKOLA TESLA

The Man Who Saw the Invisible

It was an unusually cold evening in New York City, the kind that chilled you straight through to the bone. Yet, in a small, dimly lit room on the 20th floor of the Hotel New Yorker, a single lamp illuminated a curious sight: a tall, slender man, with striking features and an air of intense concentration. He was Nikola Tesla, and his mind was anywhere but in that room.

He spent most nights like this, pouring over stacks of papers, notebooks filled with sketches, and equations scrawled with his sweeping, rapid hand. Tonight, he was lost in a vision—a vision that had haunted him for years. Tesla saw the world in a way few others did, imagining invisible forces that pulsed, circled, and whirled around him. He believed he could harness these forces to send energy across the earth without a single wire—a radical idea.

In his early years, people laughed at his ideas. Some even called him mad. But Tesla was undeterred. His mind leaped over what others called "impossible," reaching for something greater. He had brought electric light to cities, harnessed the power of Niagara Falls, and introduced the world to alternating current, the very backbone of modern electricity. But these were mere stepping stones. Tesla had much grander plans.

As he sketched a new design, his hand trembled slightly. He was imagining a tower—a massive structure that would send waves of energy through the air, wirelessly lighting up homes across continents. He called it the Wardenclyffe Tower. With it, he believed he could provide free energy to the world.

"Imagine," Tesla once said to a young reporter, who had come to interview him, "a world where no one suffers for lack of power. No coal smoke, no wires cluttering the sky, just energy as natural as sunlight. It would be a new era."

The reporter was mesmerized, though he understood little of Tesla's theories. Tesla's ideas were impossible to most, like trying to touch a star in the night sky.

But then came the darker days. Tesla's supporters withdrew, his funds dried up, and the Wardenclyffe Tower was abandoned. Though the world would go on to celebrate men like Edison, Tesla, the true visionary, was left alone, his genius slipping into obscurity.

And yet, on that cold evening in New York, as Tesla looked out of his window into the dark night, his eyes were far from defeated. He saw a future he knew he wouldn't live to see but that he believed in with every fibre of his being. It was a future where people would travel the world in seconds, communicate instantly across vast oceans, and use forces once thought to be beyond reach.

"I may not see it," he murmured, "but I know it will come to be."

Nikola Tesla revolutionized modern electricity by pioneering alternating current (AC), a system that contrasts with the previously dominant direct current (DC). AC electricity rapidly changes direction, switching between positive and negative charges multiple times per second, unlike DC, which flows steadily in one direction.

This innovation allowed electricity to travel vast distances with minimal energy loss, addressing the inefficiencies of DC. Tesla introduced transformers to easily increase or decrease voltage, enabling the safe transmission of high-voltage electricity over long distances for use in homes and businesses.

Today, AC electricity is the backbone of electrical grids, fueling homes, schools, factories, and cities while being safer and more cost-effective for large-scale energy systems. Although Tesla died alone, his legacy endures in every flicker of light and pulse of electricity

Thanks to Tesla's vision and inventions, alternating current became the standard, beating out Thomas Edison's DC system in what's famously known as the **"War of the Currents."**

So, when you turn on a light, use an appliance, or charge your devices, you're benefiting from Nikola Tesla's AC electricity system!

JAMES CLERK MAXWELL

The Weaver of Light and Magnetism

In the quiet halls of Marischal College, Aberdeen, a young man was immersed in an experiment, his fingers deftly adjusting a coil of copper wire as he gazed through a lens with intense focus. James Clerk Maxwell, a modest Scotsman with a curious mind and a love for poetry, was about to change the very foundation of science.

Maxwell's life was defined by a hunger for understanding the natural world. In his early years, he would wander the Scottish hills and sketch curious observations about the colours of the sky and the ripples in water. His mother cultivated his curiosity, and by the time he was a teenager, Maxwell was undertaking complex mathematics that left his tutors astounded.

But it was in his early thirties, while pondering the nature of light and electromagnetism, that Maxwell began to see a pattern no one else had seen. At that time, electricity and magnetism were known forces, but no one had ever suspected they were connected. Maxwell was the first to realize that light itself might be a wave—an electromagnetic wave moving at a speed astonishingly close to that of light.

He poured his discovery into a set of four equations—simple on the surface but vast in their implications. These equations, which would come to be known as "Maxwell's Equations," unified electricity, magnetism, and light into a single theory. It was as though he had woven a painting out of the invisible threads of the universe, connecting forces once thought separate.

As he finished his work, he stood back and realized the enormity of what he had uncovered. Light, electricity, and magnetism were different expressions of the same phenomenon. Maxwell understood that he was seeing something thoughtful—the very unity of nature.

Yet, like many great thinkers, Maxwell's discovery was slow to be fully appreciated. Some scientists found his ideas too abstract; others were simply unable to comprehend the beauty of his equations. He was a quiet man, preferring his calculations to public praise. But Maxwell never doubted the importance of his work.

When he completed his final paper, Maxwell offered only a humble explanation to his colleagues. "This is merely a theoretical exploration," he said, though he knew it was much more. He was opening a door to the future—a future in which his equations would inspire a new era of physics, leading to radio waves, relativity, and quantum mechanics.

James Clerk Maxwell passed away young, but his equations continued to live on, revealing truths about our world that Maxwell could only imagine. To this day, his work lights the path for scientists and engineers, his vision of unity forever etched into the very fabric of modern science.

ROSALIND FRANKLIN

The Woman Who Saw the Secret of Life

Chemist whose work with X-ray diffraction was critical to understanding the structure of DNA.

The Woman Who Saw the Secret of Life

In the dimly lit lab of **King's College London**, a determined woman stood bent over a microscope, her eyes focused on a delicate X-ray image. The image, like a puzzle, was there for the solving. Each fibre and curve held a secret—**the structure of life itself**—and **Rosalind Franklin** was determined to uncover it.

Born on **July 25, 1920**, in London, Rosalind Franklin was a brilliant and meticulous scientist whose work would go on to change the course of biology forever. From an early age, she was known for her sharp intellect and fierce determination. She was educated at **Newnham College, Cambridge**, where she studied chemistry, and her curiosity about the natural world was insatiable. But it was her work in X-ray crystallography that would lead her to one of the greatest discoveries of the 20th century: the **structure of DNA**.

In the early 1950s, Franklin was hired to work at **King's College** to study the molecular structure of DNA. Armed with her expert knowledge of X-ray diffraction techniques, she was able to capture incredibly detailed photographs of DNA molecules. Among her most famous images was **Photo 51**, an X-ray image that clearly showed the **helical structure** of DNA—an image that would prove pivotal in solving the mystery of heredity.

But Franklin's contributions were largely overlooked at the time. The discovery of the double helix structure of DNA is often attributed to **James Watson**, **Francis Crick**, and **Maurice Wilkins**, with Watson and Crick famously using **Photo 51** without Rosalind's permission. The men had access to her work through their colleague, Wilkins, and while they published their groundbreaking paper in 1953, it was Franklin who had provided the crucial evidence.

Franklin was known for her **attention to detail** and her uncompromising standards, which often led to tension with her male colleagues, especially Wilkins. She was determined not just to make a discovery, but to understand the full, intricate picture. Her persistence and thoroughness were essential to the understanding of DNA, yet she did not receive the recognition she deserved in her lifetime.

Rosalind's story is one of quiet brilliance, overshadowed at the time by the scientific community's biases. But her legacy has grown in the years since. As researchers and historians have revisited the history of DNA, it has become increasingly clear that Franklin's work was central to the discovery of the double helix. Her **precise measurements** and **meticulous observations** laid the foundation for Watson and Crick's work, but she was not part of the famous Nobel Prize awarded to them in 1962, since she had passed away in 1958 from **ovarian cancer** at the age of 37.

Yet, in her short life, Rosalind Franklin's contributions were invaluable. **Her photos, her calculations, her insights** were the bedrock upon which the modern understanding of genetics was built. It was Franklin vho, with her unique talent and unyielding dedication, evealed to the world the shape of the very molecule that nakes us who we are.

Today, Franklin is remembered not only as a brilliant cientist but also as a symbol of resilience and **undying edication** to truth in science. Her work continues to inspire vomen in science and in all fields where knowledge is ower, showing the world that sometimes the greatest ontributions are made by those who do not seek fame or ecognition, but who simply seek to know the truth.

Rosalind Franklin once said, **"Science and veryday life cannot and should not be separated."** Her fe was a testament to this idea, and her legacy lives on in very discovery that builds on the foundation she helped lay.

STEPHEN HAWKING

'he Mind that Shaped the Stars

In the quiet of a small room in Oxford, a young boy amed Stephen Hawking sat at his desk, his eyes fixed on ne night sky. The stars above seemed to whisper secrets of ne universe, of things far greater than anything he could rasp. But Stephen was determined to understand. Even as a hild, he had known that the universe wasn't just a collection f twinkling lights—it was a puzzle waiting to be solved.

Stephen was born on **January 8, 1942**, in Oxford, ngland, into a family that valued education and intellectual uriosity. His father, Frank, was a researcher in medicine, nd his mother, Isobel, worked as a research secretary. From a young age, Stephen showed a rare aptitude for mathematics and science, though he wasn't always the best student. In fact, his early academic journey was filled with frustration and self-doubt. But the spark of curiosity never left him.

He eventually attended **University College, Oxford**, where he studied physics. It was during this time that something strange began to happen. At the age of 21, while still in the prime of his academic life, Stephen started to lose control of his body. His hands trembled. His legs weakened. A visit to the doctor led to the devastating diagnosis: **amyotrophic lateral sclerosis**—ALS, a neurodegenerative disease that would slowly paralyze him. The doctors gave him only two years to live.

But Stephen wasn't one to accept fate without a fight. Instead of retreating from his studies, he dove into them deeper than ever before. The disease may have stolen his body, but it could never take away his mind. It was this unyielding resolve that would define the rest of his life.

As Stephen's body grew weaker, his mind grew stronger. At **Cambridge University**, where he continued his research in cosmology, he made a discovery that would change the course of science forever. In 1974, he proposed that black holes, once thought to be completely inescapable, could emit radiation. This radiation, which came to be known as **Hawking radiation**, challenged the very nature of black holes and sent ripples through the scientific community. His theory suggested that black holes were not the cosmic vacuums that swallowed everything in their path, but rather entities that could slowly lose mass and eventually evaporate.

Stephen's discovery was revolutionary. It bridged the gap between the two great pillars of physics—**general relativity** and **quantum mechanics**—which had never been successfully reconciled before. But despite the tributes, the recognition, and the praise, Stephen's life was far from easy.

ALS continued to progress, and by the time he was in his thirties, he was confined to a wheelchair. His speech became slurred, and soon, he could no longer speak at all. Yet, Stephen's determination never wavered. He relied on a **speech-generating device** controlled by the movement of his cheek, and with this technology, he continued to lecture, write, and communicate with the world. It was this incredible resilience in the face of such immense physical challenges that became just as remarkable as his scientific achievements.

Stephen's personal life was equally complex. In 1965, he married **Jane Wilde**, a fellow student, and they had three children together. But as the years passed, the strain of caring for a husband with a devastating illness took its toll. After 25 years, Stephen and Jane divorced, though they remained close. In 1995, he married **Elaine Mason**, one of his nurses, but this marriage too ended in divorce in 2006.

Yet, even as his personal life faced challenges, Stephen remained driven by his work. His fame grew, especially after the publication of his bestselling book, *A Brief History of Time*, in 1988. The book, which explained complex concepts of black holes, the Big Bang, and the nature of the universe in language accessible to the public, became a global sensation. It brought Stephen's genius into the homes of millions and made him a household name.

But despite the fame, Stephen remained focused on the questions that had first drawn him to science: What is the nature of time? What is the origin of the universe? And perhaps most importantly, what is the fate of humankind? His work on **cosmology** was not just theoretical—it was deeply personal. He believed that understanding the universe could help humanity survive its own future.

Stephen's thoughts turned to space exploration. In interviews and lectures, he often spoke of the need for humanity to colonize other planets. With the threat of climate change, nuclear war, and the rise of artificial intelligence, he saw space as a potential refuge for mankind. **"We are just an advanced breed of monkeys on a minor planet of a very average star. But we can understand the universe. That makes us something very special,"** he once said.

Despite the physical limitations imposed by ALS, Stephen Hawking's mind soared through the stars, unravelling the mysteries of the cosmos with a determination that inspired millions. His work bridged the gap between the known and the unknown, between the finite and the infinite.

When Stephen passed away on **March 14, 2018**, at the age of 76, the world mourned the loss of a visionary. But his legacy—his scientific contributions, his resilience, and his enduring belief that the human spirit could overcome the greatest of challenges—lives on.

Stephen Hawking had once said, **"However difficult life may seem, there is always something you can do and succeed at."** His life was a testament to that belief. He proved that even when your body is frail, your mind can reach for the stars—and beyond.

STEVE JOBS

The Visionary Who Changed the World

In the world of technology, few names resonate as strongly as Steve Jobs. Born on February 24, 1955, in San Francisco, California, Jobs was adopted by Paul and Clara Jobs, who encouraged his curiosity from an early age. He grew up in Silicon Valley, where he was exposed to the budding tech culture that would later shape his life.

Jobs was a natural-born innovator but not always an academic success. After dropping out of Reed College in Oregon, he journeyed to India in search of spiritual enlightenment, returning home with a renewed sense of purpose. In 1976, at the age of 21, Jobs co-founded Apple with Steve Wozniak and Ronald Wayne in his parents' garage. Wozniak, a gifted engineer, designed the Apple I, while Jobs handled marketing and vision, eventually turning the venture into a tech powerhouse.

The success of the Apple II, one of the first highly successful mass-produced personal computers, set the stage for Apple's future. However, Jobs was never satisfied with good enough; he was driven by an obsession with design, functionality, and user experience. This ambition led to the creation of the Macintosh in 1984, a revolutionary computer that emphasized graphical user interfaces and ease of use.

But Jobs' journey wasn't without setbacks. In 1985, after a series of clashes with Apple's board and then-CEO John Sculley, Jobs was ousted from the company he had built. Instead of giving up, Jobs used this setback to fuel new ventures. He founded NeXT, a computer platform development company, and acquired Pixar, a small animation company, which eventually became a massive success with films like *Toy Story*.

In 1997, Apple was struggling, and Jobs was invited back to save the company. He returned, bringing with him the bold ideas and revolutionary designs that Apple needed to survive. He slashed unnecessary projects and focused on simplicity and elegance. This led to the birth of the iMac, the iPod, the iPhone, and the iPad, all of which became iconic products that transformed the tech industry.

Jobs' legacy isn't just about products; it's about the relentless pursuit of perfection. He demanded excellence from his teams and himself, pushing boundaries and setting new standards in technology and design. He encouraged people to "Think Different" and inspired a generation to believe in the power of creativity and innovation.

On October 5, 2011, Steve Jobs passed away, but his vision lives on through Apple and the countless ways his work has shaped modern technology. His story is a testament to resilience, creativity, and the belief that even a small team, with a clear vision, can change the world.

Why did Steve Jobs Visit India?

Jobs visited India in 1974, when he was in his early twenties, searching for spiritual enlightenment. At that time, he was deeply interested in Eastern philosophy, meditation, and the idea of finding a higher purpose. Jobs was particularly influenced by the teachings of Zen Buddhism, and he hoped to explore and experience these spiritual practices firsthand.

He travelled to India with a friend, Daniel Kottke, who later became one of the first employees of Apple. Jobs went to visit various holy sites and gurus, including the famous Neem Karoli Baba's ashram in the foothills of the Himalayas. Jobs sought answers to life's deeper questions and hoped that his journey would provide him with clarity and peace of mind.

1. **Spiritual Insight**: Jobs didn't stay in India for long (around 7 months), but the experience had a profound effect on him. The trip deepened his interest in meditation, simplicity, and a minimalist lifestyle. His immersion in Eastern spiritual practices influenced his approach to design and life, emphasizing focus, simplicity, and intuition.

2. **A Shift in Perspective**: Jobs later reflected on how India helped him gain a clearer perspective on life, setting him on a path of deeper self-awareness. The trip to India helped him see the value of living authentically and following one's instincts, rather than following the conventional paths expected by society.

3. **Design Philosophy**: His experiences in India also influenced his later work at Apple. Jobs' appreciation for simplicity and elegance in design can be traced back to his exposure to minimalist art and philosophy in India. The idea of creating products that are beautiful and easy to use became a hallmark of Apple's products, like the iPhone and MacBook.

4. **Sense of Purpose**: The visit solidified Jobs' desire to create products that would change the world and have a meaningful impact on people's lives. His time in India allowed him to connect with a deeper sense of purpose that would later drive his innovation at Apple.

In essence, Jobs' journey to India was about searching for something beyond material success. It played a key role in shaping the person he became—both as a businessman and as a visionary. His exposure to Indian spirituality and philosophy helped him find clarity and focus, which contributed to the development of the groundbreaking products that Apple would later create.

ALEXANDER GRAHAM BELL

The Man Who Made the World Hear

In the late 19th century, few inventors matched the curiosity and creativity of Alexander Graham Bell. Born on March 3, 1847, in Edinburgh, Scotland, Bell was surrounded by a family deeply committed to the study of sound. His father and grandfather were pioneers in elocution and speech training, and his mother was deaf, which greatly influenced Bell's lifelong dedication to communication and hearing.

As a young man, Bell moved with his family to Canada in 1870 and later settled in Boston, where he taught at schools for the deaf. He developed new teaching methods and devices to help his students communicate, gaining a reputation as an innovative educator. But Bell's curiosity didn't end there; he dreamed of creating a device that could transmit sound over long distances.

In 1874, while experimenting with ways to send multiple telegraph messages over a single wire, Bell became fascinated with the possibility of transmitting voice. Working with his assistant, Thomas Watson, he tested a device that could convert sound waves into electrical signals, allowing them to be carried over wires and heard on the other end. On March 10, 1876, in a small Boston workshop, Bell made history. He famously called out to Watson, "Mr. Watson, come here, I want to see you!" Watson heard him through the experimental device, marking the world's first successful telephone transmission.

Bell's invention revolutionized communication. Soon after, he formed the Bell Telephone Company, which rapidly grew as demand for telephones spread across the United States and beyond. Within just a few years, telephones became a household necessity, forever altering how people connected over long distances.

However, Bell's interests extended far beyond the telephone. Throughout his life, he pursued numerous scientific endeavours, from aeronautics and hydrofoils to exploring the possibilities of human-powered flight. His spirit of curiosity never waned, and he held over 30 patents for various inventions.

Bell passed away on August 2, 1922, at his home in Nova Scotia, Canada. As a final tribute, every phone across North America was silenced for a minute on the day of his funeral, a testament to the profound impact of his invention. Alexander Graham Bell's legacy endures not only in the devices that keep us connected but also in the spirit of innovation he championed. His story is one of boundless curiosity and the belief that sound could bridge worlds, allowing voices to reach across distances as never before.

TIM BERNERS LEE

Inventor of the World Wide Web

The digital age owes much to one man: Tim Berners-Lee. Born on June 8, 1955, in London, England, Berners-Lee was raised in a household fascinated by computing. Both his parents were early computer scientists, and their enthusiasm for technology inspired young Tim to pursue a career that would eventually reshape modern life.

In the 1980s, Berners-Lee worked as a software engineer at CERN, the European Organization for Nuclear Research, in Switzerland. Researchers at CERN, as well as scientists worldwide, needed a way to share and access information quickly, but existing communication methods were insufficient and complex. Recognizing this problem, Berners-Lee intended a system that could link information through a series of "hypertext" documents, accessible from any location.

In 1989, Berners-Lee proposed a revolutionary idea: the World Wide Web. He designed a system of hyperlinks that allowed documents stored on different servers to be interconnected, and he developed the first web browser and editor, known as "WorldWideWeb". By 1991, the World Wide Web was live, allowing users to access and link to various resources across different servers.

What is World Wide Web(WWW)?

WWW is a system of interconnected documents and multimedia, is now a global platform for communication, commerce, and more.

Websites, hosted on servers, consist of web pages with text, images, videos, and links. The Web uses HTTP for data transfer, accessed via browsers like Chrome, Firefox, and Safari.

Key components include:

- Websites: Collections of related web pages identified by URLs.
- Web Pages: HTML documents with multimedia content.
- Links: Clickable elements that connect web pages.
- Web Browser: Software for accessing web pages.
- Web Servers: Computers storing and delivering web pages.
- URLs: Unique web addresses for web pages.

The Web runs on the internet, a global network connecting everything. It has revolutionized information access, communication, and online services. Web 2.0 and Web 3.0 technologies continue to shape its future. In essence, the World Wide Web is an ever-evolving system that has transformed how we interact with information and each other, commonly referred to as "the internet."

In summary, the **World Wide Web** is a massive system of interconnected websites and resources that has transformed the way people interact with information and each other. It's what most people refer to when they talk about "the internet."

The impact was immediate and profound. Berners-Lee's creation simplified information-sharing, democratized access to knowledge, and paved the way for modern internet culture. From news and education to social media and entertainment, nearly every aspect of life was transformed by the web's reach.

Despite the potential for profit, Berners-Lee insisted on keeping the web open and free for everyone. He founded the World Wide Web Consortium (W3C) to set standards for web development and ensure that the web remained accessible and interoperable. His vision of a decentralized, open internet would become foundational to the web's global growth.

Tim Berners-Lee's story is a reminder of the power of selflessness in innovation. His decision to give the web to the world without seeking personal gain helped create one of the most transformative inventions of all time. Thanks to his vision, billions today are connected in ways once unimaginable, united by a world just a click away.

THE WRIGHT BROTHERS

Dreamers Who Taught the World to Fly

In the early 20th century, a pair of brothers from Dayton, Ohio, would change the course of history with their vision of human flight. Wilbur and Orville Wright, born in 1867 and 1871 respectively, shared a passion for mechanics and a curiosity about the natural world from an early age. Raised in a household that encouraged exploration and education, the brothers were avid tinkerers and natural engineers.

Their fascination with flight began in childhood when their father gifted them a small toy helicopter, which sparked their imaginations and fueled their desire to build something that could carry a human into the sky. In adulthood, they went into business together, opening a bicycle shop. It was through this shop that they honed the mechanical skills and engineering insights that would become critical in their experiments with flight.

By the late 1890s, the Wright brothers were captivated by the idea of powered flight, inspired by the work of aviation pioneers like Otto Lilienthal. Unlike many of their contemporaries, Wilbur and Orville believed that achieving controlled flight required not just power but also an understanding of aerodynamics and balance. They set out to solve these problems with a methodical, scientific approach, meticulously studying how birds flew and testing various wing designs.

In 1903, after years of testing gliders and developing a revolutionary system for controlling the aircraft's pitch, roll, and gape, the Wright brothers were ready to attempt powered flight. On December 17, 1903, near Kitty Hawk, North Carolina, Orville piloted their machine, the *Wright Flyer*, for 12 seconds, covering a distance of 120 feet. Three more flights followed that day, with the longest lasting 59 seconds. Humanity's age-old dream of flying had finally become a reality.

Their invention was ground-breaking, but the brothers remained humble and persistent in improving their designs. They returned to Dayton and continued experimenting, eventually creating planes capable of longer, higher, and more controlled flights. In the years that followed, they demonstrated their flying machines to audiences worldwide and gained recognition from governments and industries.

The Wright brothers' success was not merely a triumph of engineering; it was a testament to patience, resilience, and the pursuit of knowledge. Their achievements opened the door to modern aviation, transforming travel, commerce, and warfare. By turning dreams of flight into reality, they taught humanity that the skies, once unreachable, could be conquered through determination and innovation.

BILL GATES

The Man Who Revolutionized Personal Computing

Founder of Microsoft Company

Bill Gates, one of the most influential figures in the history of technology, was born on October 28, 1955, in Seattle, Washington. From a young age, Gates demonstrated an extraordinary aptitude for mathematics and an insatiable curiosity about computers. His parents, recognizing his potential, encouraged his academic pursuits, enrolling him in the prestigious Lakeside School, where he was introduced to his first computer.

It was at Lakeside that Gates met Paul Allen, a fellow computer enthusiast. The two became fast friends, bonding over their shared passion for programming. They spent countless hours working on the school's computer, developing their skills and dreaming of the possibilities that computers could offer. By the time Gates graduated from high school, he was already an accomplished programmer.

In 1973, Gates enrolled at Harvard University, but his heart remained with computers. In 1975, he and Allen seized a remarkable opportunity: they saw an article about the Altair 8800, a microcomputer kit. Sensing a market for software, the duo developed a version of the BASIC programming language for the Altair. Their success with this project led them to drop out of college and form Microsoft, a company dedicated to developing software for personal computers.

Under Gates' leadership, Microsoft achieved its first major breakthrough in 1980 when it secured a contract with

IBM to provide an operating system for its new personal computer. Gates and his team quickly purchased a simple operating system from another company, modified it, and presented it as MS-DOS. This deal was transformative, establishing Microsoft as a dominant player in the emerging personal computer industry.

Gates' vision extended beyond just operating systems. He foresaw a future where personal computers would be ubiquitous, accessible, and user-friendly. This vision led to the development of Microsoft Windows, an operating system with a graphical user interface that made computers easier to use for the average person. Launched in 1985, Windows revolutionized personal computing, and subsequent versions of the software became integral to the growth of the PC market.

Throughout the 1990s, Microsoft expanded its product line, introducing software like Microsoft Office, which became the standard for productivity applications. Gates' relentless drive and keen business acumen helped Microsoft grow into one of the world's most valuable companies, making him one of the richest people in the world.

Despite his immense success, Gates' ambitions were not solely focused on business. In 2000, he and his then-wife, Melinda, founded the Bill & Melinda Gates Foundation, one of the largest private philanthropic organizations in the world. The foundation focuses on global health, education, and poverty alleviation, aiming to improve the lives of millions of people around the globe.

Bill Gates' story is one of extraordinary vision, innovation, and philanthropy. From his early days as a computer whiz to his role as a pioneering entrepreneur and a leading philanthropist, Gates has left an indelible mark on the world. His contributions to technology and society exemplify the profound impact that one individual can have through dedication, creativity, and a commitment to making the world a better place.

12. Nursing:

"The Healing Touch: The Evolution of Nursing Through the Ages"

FLORENCE NIGHTINGALE

The Woman Who Revolutionized Modern Nursing

An English social reformer and the founder of modern nursing. Her efforts during the Crimean War and her subsequent work in public health and hospital reform have left a lasting legacy in the medical field.

Florence Nightingale, born on May 12, 1820, in Florence, Italy, was a pioneering figure in nursing and healthcare reform. The second daughter of wealthy British parents, she was named after her birthplace. Nightingale's early education was unconventional for a woman of her time, as her father, William Nightingale, provided her with a thorough grounding in mathematics, philosophy, and classical languages. This education would later serve her well in her meticulous approach to healthcare.

Despite societal expectations that she marry and settle into domestic life, Nightingale felt a divine calling to serve others, particularly through nursing. In the early 1840s, she began to pursue her interest in healthcare, studying hospitals in London and Paris. Her resolve was strengthened by visits to religious institutions in Egypt and Germany, where she observed different approaches to healthcare and hygiene.

Nightingale's most significant contribution came during the Crimean War (1853–1856). Appalled by reports of the appalling conditions faced by wounded British soldiers, she volunteered her services and was appointed to oversee nursing at the military hospital in Scutari, Turkey. Arriving with a team of 38 nurses in 1854, she found soldiers suffering in filth, with inadequate supplies, poor sanitation, and widespread disease.

Implementing strict hygiene practices and reorganizing the hospital's management, Nightingale drastically reduced the death rate. Her use of statistical analysis to demonstrate the impact of sanitary reforms was ground-breaking. She meticulously documented the causes of mortality, using data to advocate for systemic changes in military and civilian hospitals. This earned her the nickname "The Lady with the Lamp," as she was often seen making rounds at night, providing care and comfort to the soldiers.

Throughout her life, Nightingale suffered from various health problems, worsened by her work during the Crimean War. She contracted "Crimean fever" (likely a form of brucellosis) and was often bedridden, yet she continued to work on healthcare reforms and nursing education from her bed.

Upon returning to England after the war, Nightingale continued her mission to reform healthcare. Nightingale faced bureaucratic obstacles while advocating for healthcare reforms. Navigating the complex political and administrative systems to push for changes in the British Army's medical services and public health policies required meticulous data collection and persuasive communication to overcome institutional inertia. Her single-minded dedication to her work often left her isolated, distancing her from family and many contemporaries. She had to rely on a small circle of close friends and allies for support.

Establishing the Nightingale Training School for Nurses and other healthcare initiatives required significant financial resources and logistical planning. Nightingale had to secure funding, develop curricula, and ensure the successful operation of these institutions amidst various constraints. Despite these challenges, Florence Nightingale's unwavering commitment to improving healthcare and her pioneering spirit enabled her to make lasting contributions to the field of nursing and public health, with her legacy continuing to inspire healthcare professionals worldwide.

In 1860, she founded the Nightingale Training School for Nurses at St. Thomas' Hospital in London, establishing nursing as a respected profession. Her book, "Notes on Nursing: What It Is and What It Is Not," became an important text in nursing education, emphasizing the importance of sanitation, patient observation, and compassion.

Nightingale's influence extended beyond nursing. She was instrumental in reforming the British Army's medical services and improving public health in India, using her statistical skills to advocate for better sanitary conditions. Despite being bedridden with illness for much of her later life, Nightingale remained an active and influential figure, corresponding with leaders and continuing her advocacy through writing and advising.

Florence Nightingale passed away on August 13, 1910, at the age of 90. Her legacy endures in the form of modern nursing practices, healthcare reform, and the professionalization of nursing. She is remembered not only for her practical contributions to medicine but also for her compassionate care and relentless pursuit of better healthcare for all.

CLARA BARTON

The founder of American Red Cross

Founder of the American Red Cross, Clara Barton provided essential care to soldiers during the American Civil War. Her efforts in organizing field hospitals and assisting in disaster relief laid the foundation for modern emergency response and disaster nursing.

Clara Barton, born on December 25, 1821, in North Oxford, Massachusetts, was a pioneering nurse, humanitarian, and founder of the American Red Cross. Known as the "Angel of the Battlefield" for her courageous work during the American Civil War, Barton provided critical medical care and supplies directly on the front lines, often in challenging and dangerous conditions. Her compassionate and determined spirit led her to advocate for the rights and care of soldiers, and she organized efforts to reunite missing soldiers with their families after the war.

In 1881, inspired by her work in Europe with the International Red Cross, she established the American Red Cross, focusing on disaster relief and emergency response. Clara Barton's legacy endures through her lasting contributions to nursing, emergency medicine, and humanitarian work, establishing her as one of the most influential figures in American medical history.

There's a captivating story about Clara Barton's resilience and ingenuity during the Civil War—one that feels like a narrative:

The Missing Soldier's Letter

It was late in the evening, and Clara Barton sat by the dim light of a lantern in her makeshift office. The war had ended, but her mission was far from over. A stack of letters lay before her, each one filled with desperation and hope from families searching for loved ones who had vanished during the war.

One letter, in particular, caught her attention. It was from a grieving mother in Ohio who hadn't heard from her son, Private James Caldwell, in two years. The woman described her son's last known location and begged for news. Clara could feel the anguish in every word. Determined to help, she began her investigation.

A Trail of Clues

Clara had already gained permission from President Abraham Lincoln to establish the **Office of Missing Soldiers**, a network dedicated to locating soldiers who were missing in action. She reviewed every record she had, cross-referencing the mother's description with casualty lists and prisoner-of-war rosters.

Weeks turned into months, but Clara didn't give up. She eventually found a clue—a fellow soldier recalled seeing James Caldwell taken to Andersonville Prison, the infamous Confederate camp known for its horrific conditions. It wasn't much, but it was enough to rekindle her determination.

The Breakthrough

Clara began writing letters to former Andersonville prisoners, asking if anyone had known James Caldwell. At last, a reply came. A soldier remembered James—he had fallen gravely ill in the camp but had shown remarkable courage, sharing his meager rations with weaker comrades. Sadly, the soldier confirmed that James had passed away in the camp.

Though the news was heartbreaking, Clara wrote to the grieving mother with as much compassion as she could muster. She shared details of her son's bravery and kindness, ensuring that his memory would live on as a hero.

A Lasting Impact

This story was not unique in Clara's work; she helped identify over 22,000 missing soldiers during her lifetime, bringing closure to thousands of families. Through her relentless efforts, she became a beacon of hope for the heartbroken, proving that even in the darkest times, acts of kindness and determination could light the way.

This story reflects not just her dedication but also her ingenuity in navigating the challenges of post-war America. It's a testament to Clara Barton's enduring legacy as a humanitarian and a hero.

MARY ELIZA MAHONEY

Pioneer of Professional Nursing

Mary Eliza Mahoney, born in 1845 in Dorchester, Massachusetts, holds the distinction of being the first African American woman to become a registered nurse in the United States. Graduating from the rigorous program at the New England Hospital for Women and Children in 1879, Mahoney was a dedicated and skilled nurse, highly respected for her commitment to patient care. She faced significant racial and gender barriers but remained steadfast in her pursuit of excellence, advocating for equal opportunities for African American nurses.

Mahoney co-founded the National Association of Colored Graduate Nurses (NACGN) in 1908, promoting professional growth and creating a support network for Black nurses. Her pioneering work and dedication to equality in healthcare inspired generations, establishing her as a trailblazer in nursing and civil rights.

LILLIAN WAILD

Visionary of Public Health and Advocate for Social Reform

Lillian Wald, born on March 10, 1867, in Cincinnati, Ohio, was a leader in public health nursing and a passionate social reformer. Recognizing the need for healthcare among New York City's underserved populations, she founded the Henry Street Settlement in 1893, offering nursing services and social support to immigrant communities on the Lower East Side. Wald advocated for healthcare as a fundamental human right and was instrumental in shaping the role of nurses in public health.

Her work extended beyond nursing, as she championed child labour laws, education, and women's rights, and collaborated with government agencies to improve health standards. Known as the "Mother of Public Health Nursing," Wald's contributions laid the foundation for community nursing, making her a key figure in American healthcare and social welfare.

A knock at her door

One of the most important stories about Lillian Wald, the founder of public health nursing, began with a simple knock at her door.

In 1893, while teaching a home nursing class to immigrant women in New York City, Lillian Wald was approached by a young girl. The child, desperate and crying, begged Lillian to come and help her sick mother. Moved by the girl's plea, Lillian followed her to a tenement building on the Lower East Side.

When Lillian arrived, she found the girl's mother gravely ill, lying in a dirty, overcrowded apartment. The family, struggling with poverty, couldn't afford a doctor. Lillian quickly cared for the woman, but what struck her deeply was the terrible living condition of the family—and their neighbors.

That day, Lillian decided to dedicate her life to helping the poor, especially immigrants who had little access to healthcare. She left her wealthy lifestyle and moved into a small apartment in the Lower East Side with her friend Mary Brewster. Together, they began offering free nursing care to anyone in need, regardless of their ability to pay.

This simple act of kindness grew into something much bigger. Lillian founded the **Henry Street Settlement**, an organization that provided not only nursing services but also education, housing, and social programs for the community. Her work changed the way healthcare was delivered to the poor and helped create the field of public health nursing.

This story shows how one moment of compassion can spark a lifetime of change. Lillian's decision to help that little girl's family led to a movement that improved lives for countless people.

VIRGINIA HENDERSON

First Lady of Nursing and a Theorist of Holistic Care.

Virginia Henderson, born on November 30, 1897, in Kansas City, Missouri, was a pioneering nurse and educator who is best known for her development of the Nursing Need Theory. Often referred to as the "first lady of nursing," Henderson's work emphasized the importance of patient independence and the role of nurses in helping individuals achieve self-sufficiency.

Her theory, which identified 14 basic needs that all individuals require for health and well-being, has had a profound influence on nursing practice and education. Henderson's focus on all-inclusive care and her advocacy for the professionalization of nursing helped shape modern nursing into a patient-centered and scientifically grounded field. Throughout her career, she made significant contributions to nursing theory, research, and education, and her legacy continues to inspire the practice of nursing worldwide.

Virginia Henderson, often referred identified **14 basic human needs** that form the foundation of her **Nursing Need Theory**. These needs focus on the care required to support a person's health, recovery, or peaceful death. The needs encompass physical, psychological, spiritual, and social aspects of well-being.

Henderson's 14 Basic Needs:

1. **Breathing**: Ensuring sufficient oxygen intake for survival.

2. **Eating and Drinking**: Adequate nutrition and hydration.

3. **Elimination**: Proper excretion of bodily wastes.

4. **Posture and Movement**: Ensuring proper body position, mobility, and physical activity.

5. **Sleep and Rest**: Adéquate rest and relaxation.

6. **Clothing**: Choosing suitable clothing to maintain body temperature and dignity.

7. **Body Temperature**: Maintaining a stable body temperature.

8. **Hygiene and Grooming**: Keeping the body clean and well-groomed to protect the skin and maintain self-esteem.

9. **Avoiding Danger**: Ensuring physical safety and preventing harm to the individual.

10. **Communication**: Expressing emotions, needs, fears, or opinions effectively.

11. **Worship and Faith**: Practicing religious beliefs or engaging in spiritual practices as desired.

12. **Work and Achievement**: Feeling productive and finding purpose through work or meaningful activities.

13. **Recreation**: Engaging in hobbies or leisure activities for mental and emotional well-being.

14. **Learning and Growth**: Acquiring knowledge and developing skills for health and independence.

Her approach highlights the importance of holistic nursing, where care is tailored to meet these fundamental needs, especially when patients are unable to fulfill them independently. Nurses act as a bridge, helping individuals regain independence or ensuring comfort when independence is not possible.

JEAN WATSON

The Heart of Healing - Jean Watson

The room was filled with a soft, gentle light that seemed to infuse everything it touched with a serene warmth. There, amid the hushed bustle of nurses and doctors, sat Dr. Jean Watson, radiating calm and compassion as she listened to a patient's story, as if the world around them had fallen away.

It wasn't just her gentle presence that drew people to her; it was the way she truly saw each patient. Jean Watson's approach went beyond medicine as science—it was medicine as art. Her Theory of Human Caring transformed healthcare, reminding doctors, nurses, and caregivers everywhere that healing wasn't only about treating the body but also about touching the soul.

Jean's career had begun like any other young nurse's: full of curiosity, tempered by a sense of duty. But over the years, as she witnessed the pain and isolation that often accompanied illness, she began to see gaps in traditional care. She realized that healing required not just medicine, but empathy and human connection. Her theory, the "Theory of Human Caring," was born from this insight, and she went on to create a movement that redefined what it meant to be a nurse.

As she spoke with the patient that day, she leaned forward, her hands clasped gently in her lap, embodying the core principles she championed—presence, touch, understanding, and compassion. Jean encouraged her fellow nurses to see patients as individuals with lives, dreams, and fears, rather than mere cases or symptoms.

She shared stories of her own moments of doubt and challenge, where she had struggled to balance her scientific knowledge with her desire to nurture and comfort. It was not always easy; science could be demanding, facts rigid. But Jean had come to see that true healing lay in the middle ground, where science met the spirit. In the fusion of these two, she found a purpose so powerful it had changed the face of nursing.

In her twilight years, Jean continued to inspire students, nurses, and doctors alike. She created centers for Caring Science, published books, and travelled the world, each step further embedding her message of human caring into the fabric of healthcare. Her legacy was in the thousands of nurses who saw themselves not merely as medical practitioners but as healers, dedicated to walking beside their patients in times of suffering, joy, fear, and hope.

As Jean Watson left the patient's room, she took a moment to glance back. Her eyes held a deep wisdom and a quiet satisfaction. She knew she had done her part to bring a little more kindness into the world, one patient, one caregiver, one life at a time.

13. LITERARY FIGURES

There had been some notable literary figures who focused on themes related to human welfare, justice, and social reform in their works: These authors and thinkers highlighted social issues of their times and helped shape attitudes toward human rights, justice, and welfare through literature.

WILLIAM SHAKESPEARE

The Soul of a Poet

In the small English town of Stratford-upon-Avon, under the warm glow of the setting sun, a young William Shakespeare wandered the banks of the Avon River. The future poet and playwright was a mere teenager then, unknown to the world, yet his mind brimmed with words, stories, and characters that even he didn't fully understand.

As the eldest son of a glove-maker, William's life was destined for the same steady work, yet his mind flew beyond the simple trades of his small town. He would spend hours in solitude, listening to the sounds of birds, the murmur of the river, and the distant laughter of the townsfolk. Each sound, each scene, seemed to stir a deeper meaning in him. He noticed the little things—the sorrowful glances, the joyous dances, the shifting of the seasons—all weaving their way into his imagination.

Years passed, and Shakespeare left Stratford for the bustling city of London. The city pulsed with life, with merchants, nobles, and craftsmen filling every corner. And there, amidst the crowds of people, William found his calling in the theatre, where he could share his characters, dreams, and questions about human nature with an audience.

But it wasn't easy. There were long nights of rehearsals, fierce competition, and critics who doubted his work. Yet, even in moments of despair, when the words seemed just out of reach, he would remember the sounds of the river, the warmth of the sun in Stratford, and the familiar faces he once knew. Those memories gave him the strength to keep writing, pushing his imagination to its limits.

In time, Shakespeare's words resonated far beyond the boundaries of London. Kings and queens, scholars and commoners, all came to witness his tales. In *Hamlet*, *Macbeth*, *Romeo and Juliet*, and countless others, he asked questions about love, ambition, jealousy, and honour—questions that no one could easily answer. Through his plays, he mirrored life itself, in all its beauty and sorrow, humour and tragedy.

As he grew older, he returned to Stratford, weary yet fulfilled. His fame had grown, but he still longed for the quiet life he had once known. Sitting by the river, he would reflect on the vast worlds he had created and how his humble beginnings had somehow led him to the heart of human nature. Shakespeare knew that his words were his legacy—his gift to the world, a reminder of the shared humanity in every laugh, tear, and sigh.

Today, his words live on, as vibrant as they were when he first wrote them. In theaters across the world, his characters continue to breathe, to love, and to fight. And in each verse, each soliloquy, each tragedy and comedy, Shakespeare's voice speaks to us, reminding us that, in the end, we are all actors on the stage of life, playing our parts, bound by the same hopes, fears, and dreams.

LEO TOLSTOY

The Quest for Truth - Leo Tolstoy

On a vast estate in the Russian countryside, a young Leo Tolstoy sat alone, gazing at the boundless land stretching before him. Born into privilege, Leo had all the comforts life could offer, yet he felt a curious emptiness, a pull toward something deeper, more meaningful. The countryside around him was a beautiful contrast to the turbulent questions in his heart: Why were people unequal? What was the purpose of life?

As he grew older, Leo went to war and witnessed first-hand the horrors of violence. He saw young men, full of life, fall to the brutal realities of combat. This experience, coupled with his observations of the Russian peasantry and the suffering they endured, stayed with him, inspiring a burning need to understand the nature of humanity.

With a pen in hand, Leo poured his soul into words. He created epic novels like *War and Peace* and *Anna Karenina*, capturing the struggles and triumphs of people caught in the tides of history and fate. His stories were not just about individuals but about society itself. Through each character and scene, he questioned the nature of happiness, love, and morality.

Yet, despite his literary success, Tolstoy remained restless. In his later years, he turned to philosophy and spirituality, deeply troubled by the gap between the lives of the wealthy and the poor. Renouncing his wealth, he took on a simple life, teaching, farming, and writing works on nonviolence and compassion. He sought universal truth, writing about the power of kindness and humility.

On a cold autumn day, near the end of his life, Tolstoy left his home, seeking solace in the simplicity of nature. He passed away at a small train station, but his legacy—his search for truth, his compassion for humanity—lived on. His words became a timeless guide for people around the world, reminding them that love, humility, and the pursuit of truth are what make life worth living.

Leo Tolstoy and the Beggar's Lesson

Leo Tolstoy, the famous Russian writer, believed deeply in kindness and helping others. One day, he experienced a small but meaningful moment that taught him an important lesson about generosity.

Tolstoy was walking down the street when a beggar approached him, asking for money. Tolstoy reached into his pockets, but to his embarrassment, he realized he had no coins with him.

Feeling sorry, Tolstoy said, **"I'm so sorry, brother, I have nothing to give you."**

Instead of being upset, the beggar smiled and said, "You gave me more than money—you called me brother."

Why It's Interesting

This simple encounter left a deep impression on Tolstoy. He realized that even small gestures of respect, kindness, and human connection could have a profound impact. It reinforced his belief in treating everyone with dignity, regardless of their social status or circumstances.

This story shows how Tolstoy's compassion and humility were part of his life, not just his writings. It reminds us that sometimes, kind words and genuine respect can be as valuable as material gifts.

FYODOR DOSTOEVSKY

In the Depths of the Soul - Fyodor Dostoevsky

The Russian winter was harsh, with freezing winds that cut through everything. Fyodor Dostoevsky, a young man with sharp eyes and a passionate heart, was on his way to be executed for his political beliefs. He stood with others, waiting for what he thought were his final moments. But just as the soldiers prepared to fire, news arrived—a pardon from the Tsar had saved his life.

Instead of death, Dostoevsky was sent to a prison camp in Siberia, where he spent years among criminals and outcasts. He saw the worst sides of human nature but also found strength, faith, and traces of goodness, even in the most broken people. This life-changing experience stayed with him forever.

After his release, Dostoevsky returned to St. Petersburg, deeply affected by his experiences. He threw himself into writing, pouring his struggles and emotions into his novels. Stories like *Crime and Punishment*, *The Brothers Karamazov*, and *Notes from Underground* explored big questions about guilt, forgiveness, suffering, and the search for purpose. Through these works, he gave readers a raw and honest view of human emotions—love, jealousy, despair, and hope.

Dostoevsky's life was full of challenges. He faced poverty, epilepsy, and a serious gambling problem. Yet, these hardships inspired his writing, making it deeply relatable and full of truth. In *The Brothers Karamazov*, he wrote about faith and doubt, while in *Crime and Punishment*, he wrestled with questions of right and wrong. His stories reflected his belief that every person struggles between good and evil.

In his later years, Dostoevsky became a respected writer and thinker. His books touched people's hearts by showing that even in life's hardest moments, there is hope and a chance for redemption. Dostoevsky's journey through suffering shaped his words, offering a message that even in pain, there is meaning—and the possibility of finding peace.

Anna Grigoryevna was Fyodor Dostoevsky's second wife and a key figure who brought stability to his troubled life. They met in 1866 when Dostoevsky, under immense pressure to finish his novel *The Gambler*, hired Anna, a 20-year-old stenographer, to help him meet a tight deadline. Anna was bright, capable, and a fan of Dostoevsky's work, especially his novel *Poor Folk.*

As they worked together, Dostoevsky opened up to Anna about his struggles. He spoke of his gambling addiction, the debts weighing him down, and the grief he carried from losing his first wife and brother. Anna listened with compassion, and their professional relationship quickly turned into a deep connection.

After completing the manuscript, Dostoevsky proposed to Anna in a unique way. He described a scene in the story where the hero confesses his love and asked Anna how she thought the heroine would respond. Smiling, Anna replied, “She would say yes.” Soon after, they were married, despite their 25-year age difference and Dostoevsky’s troubled past.

Their life together was not easy. Dostoevsky’s gambling addiction often left them in financial trouble, and at times Anna had to sell her belongings to cover debts. But she remained patient and supportive, managing their finances and encouraging him to focus on his writing. Anna's practical nature brought much-needed stability to Dostoevsky’s chaotic life.

The couple traveled across Europe, living modestly while Dostoevsky worked on some of his greatest novels, including *Crime and Punishment* and *The Brothers Karamazov.* Anna also helped publish his works, negotiating with publishers and improving their financial situation over time.

After Dostoevsky’s death in 1881, Anna dedicated herself to preserving his legacy. She compiled his manuscripts, letters, and notes, ensuring his works continued to reach readers. Her memoirs give us a personal glimpse into Dostoevsky’s life and the struggles they faced together.

Anna was not just Dostoevsky’s wife but also his partner, supporter, and savior. Her love and strength helped him through his darkest times, making it possible for him to create the masterpieces we cherish today.

VICTOR HUGO

Voice of the Oppressed - Victor Hugo

Victor Hugo stood on a windy balcony, looking over the rooftops of Paris. The city, full of beauty and hardship, deeply moved him. Born during a time of wars and revolutions, Hugo had seen the struggles of ordinary people. From a young age, he knew he wanted to speak up for those who couldn't speak for themselves.

As a young poet and playwright, Hugo was drawn to ideas of freedom and justice, often challenging the strict rules of society. But it was his novels that made him famous. In *Les Misérables*, he told powerful stories about the poor and suffering, like Jean Valjean, Fantine, and the street children of Paris. He showed that poverty and crime weren't just personal failures but signs of a society failing its people.

Hugo's fight for justice didn't stop with his books. When Napoleon III came to power, Hugo openly criticized the government's injustices. His boldness forced him into exile, and for nearly 20 years, he lived away from France. Even from afar, Hugo continued to speak out, writing strongly against tyranny, the death penalty, and social injustice.

Over time, Hugo became a symbol of hope for the French people. When he returned to France, he was celebrated as a hero. Wherever he went, crowds gathered to see him, drawn by his compassion and unwavering belief in justice.

When Hugo passed away in 1885, Paris was in mourning. Thousands of people filled the streets to honor not just a great writer but a man who had dedicated his life to humanity. His legacy lives on in his stories, poems, and the hearts of those who dream of a kinder, fairer world.

A deeply touching story from Victor Hugo's personal life is the profound grief he experienced after the tragic death of his beloved daughter, Léopoldine.

Léopoldine, Hugo's eldest daughter, was the light of his life. She married Charles Vacquerie in 1843, and their happiness brought great joy to Hugo. But just a few months after her wedding, tragedy struck. While boating on the Seine River, Léopoldine and her husband were caught in an accident. Their boat capsized, and both drowned. Léopoldine was only 19 years old.

Hugo was away in the Pyrenees when he learned the devastating news. He found out in the most heartbreaking way—by reading about the accident in a newspaper at a café. The loss shattered him. He later wrote in his diary, "She was my happiness, my pride, my future. I was hers. And now she is no longer."

Overcome with grief, Hugo turned to poetry to express his sorrow. In his collection *Les Contemplations*, he poured his pain into verses that are some of the most moving reflections on love and loss in literature. In one of his most famous poems, *Demain, dès l'aube* ("Tomorrow, at Dawn"), he describes his journey to visit Léopoldine's grave. The poem's simple yet profound words capture the depth of his love and the enduring ache of her absence.

Léopoldine's death changed Hugo forever. It deepened his compassion for those who suffered loss and made him even more committed to fighting for the vulnerable and oppressed. This tragedy, though heartbreaking, became a source of inspiration for the empathy and humanity that shines through his works.

RABINDRANATH TAGORE

The Poet of Peace - Rabindranath Tagore

In a quiet room filled with warm sunlight, Rabindranath Tagore sat by the window, pen in hand, looking out at the peaceful countryside of Shantiniketan. This place was his retreat, where creativity and ideas could thrive. Born into a respected family in Bengal, Tagore grew up surrounded by literature and philosophy, but he always wanted to go beyond the usual path in life.

Tagore dreamed of a world free from hatred, ignorance, and suffering. This dream shaped everything he did. His poems, songs, and stories spoke about love, harmony, and the beauty of nature. His collection of devotional poems, *Gitanjali*, earned him the Nobel Prize in Literature, making him the first non-European to win this honor.

Despite his global fame, Tagore remained deeply connected to his roots. He founded Shantiniketan, an experimental school where learning was about freedom, creativity, and connecting with nature. Here, teachers and students from different backgrounds came together in an environment of respect and curiosity. For Tagore, education wasn't just about knowledge but about nurturing the human spirit.

As his reputation grew, Tagore used his voice to stand up for freedom. He loved India deeply and criticized British colonial rule, but his vision was bigger than just one nation. He dreamed of a world without borders, where all people could live together as one family. During his travels across continents, he shared this message of unity and left a lasting impression on everyone he met.

In his later years, Tagore continued to write, compose music, and inspire others. His songs became the heart of Bengal, and his thoughts on peace and unity touched people around the world. Even as he grew older, his words remained a source of hope and wisdom.

The Indian National Anthem was written by Rabindranath Tagore. The story behind the writing of India's national anthem, *Jana Gana Mana*, by Rabindranath Tagore is both inspiring and reflective of his deep love for the country and his artistic vision.

In 1911, during the session of the Indian National Congress in Kolkata (then Calcutta), Tagore was asked to compose a song that would reflect the spirit of the Indian people. The event was a significant one, as the Congress was calling for greater representation and rights for Indians under British rule. Tagore was already a prominent figure, known for his poetry, music, and social activism, and was keenly aware of the struggles for India's independence.

The song *Jana Gana Mana* was composed by Tagore in Bengali, drawing inspiration from the diversity and unity of India. The lyrics are a tribute to the country's vast landscapes, its rich cultures, and its people, symbolizing the idea of a united nation despite its diversity. The song was meant to evoke a sense of belonging and pride among Indians from all regions and communities.

The song was first publicly performed at the Calcutta session of the Indian National Congress on December 27, 1911. Although it was initially performed as a song of praise for the unity of the Indian people, it was later recognized for its broader appeal and power.

The full version of the song has five stanzas, but it was the first stanza that was eventually adopted as the national anthem of India in 1950, after India gained independence. The anthem was chosen for its ability to unify people from various regions, cultures, and religions, reflecting the inclusive spirit of the nation.

Interestingly, the song is often thought to be a tribute to the unity of India as a whole, but the British rulers also mistakenly interpreted the song as being directed toward King George V, during his visit to India in 1911. However, Tagore himself later clarified that the anthem was meant to represent the entire nation and its diverse people, rather than a single ruler.

The music for *Jana Gana Mana* was also composed by Tagore himself. His unique ability to blend lyrical beauty with a deep sense of patriotism made the anthem a timeless symbol of India's national identity. Today, the anthem continues to inspire millions, reminding them of the values of unity, freedom, and the shared spirit of the nation.

Tagore spent his final days quietly, writing until the end. He passed away in 1941, but his spirit lives on in his poetry, music, and the hearts of those who believe in a world united by love and humanity.

TONI MORRISON

The Voice of the Forgotten - Toni Morrison

In a small room in Ohio, Toni Morrison sat at her typewriter, the sound of the keys tapping as she wrote down her thoughts. She was a mother, a teacher, and a writer, balancing her daily life while working on a dream that would eventually change American literature. Born Chloe Anthony Wofford, she grew up in a family that loved telling stories, and this love of storytelling would shape her writing.

Morrison's early years were filled with stories about African American history, culture, and folklore, often showing the strength and resilience of her ancestors. She saw writing as a way to give voice to those who had been silenced and to share the untold stories of Black Americans. Her first novel, *The Bluest Eye*, challenged people to think about society's standards of beauty and the harm they caused.

With each new book, Morrison explored deeper topics like identity, love, and survival. Her most famous novel, *Beloved*, told the powerful story of slavery's lasting effects and the struggle to reclaim dignity. For her, writing was a way to tell the truth, to face painful histories with bravery and kindness. In 1993, she was awarded the Nobel Prize in Literature, becoming the first African American woman to win this honor. Her speech was a celebration of language's ability to heal and shape society.

Even with all her success, Morrison stayed true to her roots, focusing on telling real, human stories—stories of love, pain, and strength. She wrote with deep empathy, capturing both the darkness and the resilience in people's hearts, always showing the strength of the human spirit.

Toni Morrison's words continue to inspire readers, encouraging them to face difficult truths while holding onto hope. She passed away in 2019, but her legacy lives on, motivating new generations to value their histories, find their voices, and believe in their worth as human beings.

14.REAL HEROES

A Salute to True Heroes

This touching story of mutual respect and selflessness reminds us why these two great men are revered. They lived for others and left behind legacies of service, humility, and dedication to the nation. True heroes like Sam Manekshaw and Dr. Abdul Kalam inspire us to aim for greatness, not for personal gain, but for the betterment of others.

Dr.A.P.J. Abdul Kalam

Dr. A.P.J. Abdul Kalam, also known as the "Missile Man of India," was India's President from 2002 to 2007. He was a brilliant scientist who helped develop India's missile and nuclear programs. Before becoming President, he contributed significantly to India's space and defense research.

As President, he won everyone's heart with his simplicity, love for teaching, and passion for working with young people. He dreamt of making India a developed nation and focused on improving education and technology. Even after his presidency, he inspired millions with his books and speeches. Dr. Kalam passed away in 2015 but remains a symbol of humility, knowledge, and dedication to the nation.

Field Marshal Sam Manekshaw

Field Marshal Sam Manekshaw was one of India's greatest military leaders. He became the Chief of the Army Staff in 1969 and led the Indian Army to victory in the 1971 war with

Pakistan, which created Bangladesh. His sharp mind, fearless leadership, and smart planning were key to this success.

Manekshaw was known for his bold decisions and his ability to boost the morale of his soldiers. After independence, he played a major role in making the Indian Army strong and ready for challenges. In 1973, he became the first Indian Army officer to be awarded the rank of Field Marshal, the highest military honor. Even after retiring in 1978, he remained a respected figure for his courage, wisdom, and contributions to the nation.

When Dr. Kalam and Field Marshal Manekshaw met

Part 1:

During Dr. Kalam's presidency, he visited Coonoor and learned that Field Marshal Manekshaw was in the military hospital nearby. Despite it not being planned, Dr. Kalam decided to visit him. He spent about 15 minutes with Sam, asking about his health and well-being. Before leaving, Dr. Kalam asked, *"Are you comfortable? Is there anything I can do for you?"*

Part 2:

Sam Manekshaw replied, *"Yes, Your Excellency, I have one grievance."*

A surprised Dr. Kalam asked, *"What is it?"* Sam said, *"Sir, my grievance is that I am unable to stand up and salute my most respected President of my beloved country."*

Both men were deeply moved. Dr. Kalam held Sam's hand, and they shared a moment filled with mutual respect and tears.

Part 3:

Later, Sam revealed another concern. He had not been receiving the pension for his rank as Field Marshal for nearly 20 years. Dr. Kalam was horrified.

Part 4:

Upon returning to Delhi, Dr. Kalam immediately acted. Within a week, he ensured Sam's pension was approved along with arrears amounting to ₹1.25 crore. A special plane delivered the cheque to Sam at Wellington in Ooty, where he was unwell.

Part 5:

But Sam Manekshaw, in his characteristic generosity, donated the entire amount to the Army Relief Fund.

A Saint's Visit to Rashtrapati Bhavan

When Dr. Abdul Kalam was the President of India, he learned that Saint Sankaracharya would be visiting Rashtrapati Bhavan. Dr. Kalam wanted to ensure the Saint was given the utmost respect and asked me, his ADC (Aide-de-Camp), about the traditional way to welcome him.

I explained that I would greet the Saint at the gates and escort him inside. After thinking for a moment, Dr. Kalam asked, *"What if I welcome him myself?"* I told him, *"Sir, by doing so, you would be giving the Saint more honor than the President."* Dr. Kalam smiled quietly and didn't say more.

I then explained how we would seat the Saint. I said, *"I will bring the Saint inside, place his seat on the visitor's sofa, and ask him to sit there, while you will sit in your usual chair."* Dr. Kalam asked, *"What if I let him sit in my chair?"*

I replied, *"Sir, you would be giving the Saint more honor than the President."* Dr. Kalam smiled again but gave no further instructions.

When the Saint arrived, I was surprised to see Dr. Kalam standing at the gate himself, holding a garland and flowers. He personally welcomed the Saint, and together we walked through the grand corridors of Rashtrapati Bhavan to his office.

As per our earlier plan, I placed the Saint's seat (a tiger skin) on the visitor's sofa. To my astonishment, Dr. Kalam asked me to move it to his presidential chair instead. His gesture was simple but deeply meaningful.

Later, I asked him why he had done that. Dr. Kalam replied with a smile, *"I wanted the President's chair to be blessed by the Saint's spiritual power, so that whoever sits in it in the future will also receive those blessings."*

His words left me speechless. I said, *"Sir, you are not just a great scientist but a saint yourself."* Dr. Kalam smiled his humble, wise smile.

This unforgettable moment showed the depth of Dr. Kalam's humility, respect for spirituality, and his belief in the power of goodness.

One of the most touching stories about Dr. A.P.J. Abdul Kalam is from his time as President of India, reflecting his humility and deep respect for people from all walks of life.

During a high-profile banquet at Rashtrapati Bhavan, attended by several VIPs and dignitaries, Dr. Kalam noticed that the waitstaff and kitchen staff were working hard to ensure everything was perfect. After the dinner, instead of leaving with the guests, Dr. Kalam quietly went to the kitchen.

He thanked the staff for their efforts and then did something extraordinary—he invited all of them to sit with him and share a meal. This gesture deeply moved everyone present. It wasn't just about the food; it was about showing that every person, no matter their role, deserved respect and acknowledgment.

This simple act of kindness revealed Dr. Kalam's true character: a leader who valued humanity over hierarchy and saw greatness in every small act of service.

One personal and heartwarming event from Dr. A.P.J. Abdul Kalam's life occurred during his childhood in Rameswaram, Tamil Nadu.

Dr. Kalam grew up in a humble family. His father, Jainulabdeen, was a boat owner and imam at a local mosque, and his mother, Ashiamma, was a homemaker. Though they were not wealthy, their home was always filled with warmth and love.

As a boy, Kalam would wake up early to help his cousin distribute newspapers in the town. This job was crucial in supporting his family's income. One day, while delivering newspapers, Kalam noticed a group of fishermen struggling to repair their broken boat. Seeing their worry about losing their livelihood, young Kalam, even though tired from the morning work, rushed to his father for advice.

His father, known for his wisdom, patiently explained how teamwork and perseverance could solve any problem. He encouraged Kalam to help them. Inspired by his father's words, Kalam gathered a few neighbors to assist in repairing the boat. They worked together, and by the evening, the fishermen had their boat ready to sail.

This small yet impactful event stayed with Dr. Kalam throughout his life. It taught him the values of empathy, hard work, and the power of collective effort—values he upheld in his journey as a scientist, teacher, and leader. It also showed how deeply connected he was to his roots and his desire to help others, no matter how small the act.

****